KURT

Texas Rascals Book Four

LORI WILDE

1

"**O**h, look, your 'twin' is breaking her engagement."

"What?" Bonnie Bradford rolled back from her desk in the downtown San Antonio office she shared with her coworker, Paige Dutton, and peered over at Paige's computer. "Let me see that."

Paige scooted aside so Bonnie could see the TMZ website.

Quickly Bonnie's gaze scanned the salacious headlines: Oscar-Winning Actress Gives Hunky Hubby-To-Be The Heave-Ho. There on the screen was Bonnie's doppelganger, young starlet Elizabeth Destiny.

The actress had obviously been ambushed by paparazzi. Her expressive eyes were wide and sad. Her normally luxuriant blond hair, the exact same shade as Bonnie's own, hung in limp strands down her back. Worry lines creased Elizabeth Destiny's forehead, and her chic clothes were rumpled.

Sighing sadly, Bonnie settled back in her chair to read the article.

The impending marriage between Hollywood's hottest leading lady Elizabeth Destiny and one of America's most eligible billionaire bache-

lors, Kurt McNally, has ended quite unlike it began, with a whimper, not a bang. The much touted "match made in heaven" has ground to a halt before it ever started. Irreconcilable differences were cited as the cause for the split, though there have been plenty of rumors about the couple's real reason for separating. At a press conference held earlier this week, Ms. Destiny announced her intention to seek seclusion during this troubled period in her life. Mr. McNally could not be reached for comment.

The article continued, but feeling slightly sick to her stomach, Bonnie pushed back from Paige's computer.

"I don't believe it," Bonnie said. "Elizabeth and Kurt were so happy together. Anybody could look at their engagement photos and tell that. And I certainly don't believe the two had irreconcilable differences. Doesn't anybody believe in commitment anymore?"

Paige shook her head. "Sometimes I worry about you, Bonnie. You act as if you really *know* these people. I like movies, too, but jeez, I don't get carried away."

"In a sense, I *do* know them," Bonnie argued. "I've seen every Elizabeth Destiny movie ever made. I look so much like her; I'm often mistaken for her. I even keep a Pinterest board on her."

"See what I mean?" Paige circled a finger in the air near her temple. "Cuckoo obsession."

"I don't think making a Pinterest board means I'm obsessed, especially since I resemble Elizabeth so much. I'm just an ardent fan."

"You *are* a dead ringer for the woman," Paige mused, studying the photo of Elizabeth Destiny on her computer, and then casting a sidelong glance at Bonnie. "Maybe she is your long lost twin, and you were separated at birth. It really is uncanny how much you look alike."

Bonnie laughed. "Don't think that hasn't crossed my mind. My mother assures me I was not a twin, but I do feel a certain affinity for Elizabeth. I think she's an incredible actress."

True enough, Bonnie could not deny her lifelong fascination with film. From the time she was a small child, she liked nothing better than escaping from her mundane life at the Cineplex near her house.

She'd grown up living with her mother and her two spinster aunts, and the most exciting moments of her childhood had unfolded at the movies.

She loved the cozy, safe feeling a darkened theater evoked. The taste of buttery popcorn, cold sodas, and chocolate-covered peanuts. The feel of the cushioned seats, the rise and fall of movie soundtracks whisking her away to magical worlds where anything was possible.

There was nothing wrong with Netflix, but it couldn't compare to seeing a movie at the theater. Yes, she was most definitely a movie aficionado, and no amount of razzing from her friend could change that.

"I remember when Elizabeth and Kurt got engaged," Bonnie said. "I watched the engagement party on Entertainment Tonight. Kurt McNally is so handsome, and he's got a body made for sin." She sighed. "A completely masculine male. Every woman's fantasy. And I hear he's a nice guy to boot."

"Ah, you've got the hots for him," Paige teased.

"Yes," Bonnie confessed, chagrined. "I know it's silly, but every time I see a picture of him, I can't help imagining what it might feel like to have him wrap those big, strong arms around me."

"He is one fine hunk of man," Paige agreed, eyeing Kurt's picture on her screen. "But aren't you a little old for puppy dog crushes?"

"I don't have a crush on him. I just appreciate his hotness.

I can't imagine what problems he and Elizabeth could have had. They seemed like a storybook couple."

"Just goes to show happy endings aren't what they're cracked up to be." Paige picked up a nail file and buffed her fingernails.

"Cynic."

"I prefer to think of myself as a realist."

"I still believe in love at first sight and happily ever after."

"That's because you've never been married."

"True. But I'd love to try it someday." Bonnie sighed again. "If only I could meet Mr. Right."

"How do you expect to meet someone if you never go out? You're way too shy. Instead of running off to the movies, you should be hitting the dating apps. You're never going to have a romance of your own hiding out in a dark theater."

"I know, but I have such a hard time talking to men. I wish I could be like Elizabeth, confident and self-assured."

"Remember," Paige admonished. "She's an actress and probably just as terrified of social situations as you are. She merely acts the part. Next time you meet a guy, try pretending you *are* Elizabeth Destiny."

"I don't know," Bonnie hedged. "Do you really think it would work?"

"You're a beautiful woman, Bradford. I wish I had half your looks. Why do you insist on hiding your figure in frumpy clothes, keeping your hair in a bun, and wearing glasses instead of getting Lasik eye surgery? You need to live a little. Hell, why don't you start dressing like Elizabeth Destiny? If you'd let your hair down once in a while, you'd have to beat the men off with a stick."

Bonnie blushed. "I don't *want* to beat men off with a stick. I just want to fall in love, get married, and raise a family."

"Then come to the *Fast Lane* with me and Kelly tonight," Paige said, referring to a nightclub she frequented.

"Not tonight." Bonnie wrinkled her nose. She hated drinking and loud clubs and suave, insincere men delivering flattery in hopes of luring inebriated females into their beds.

"You'll never change," Paige predicted, closing the TMZ website. "Once an introvert, always an introvert, I suppose."

Was it silly for her to feel so saddened over a movie star's broken engagement? "It's such a shame about Elizabeth and Kurt. I wish there were something I could do to save their relationship."

"That's your problem, Bonnie. You're too kindhearted. Always worrying about saving the world when you should be taking care of business." Paige glanced at her watch. "Hey, it's five o'clock, and I'm outta here. You coming?"

"I've got some letters to finish for Mr. Briggs." Bonnie waved a hand at her keyboard. "You go ahead."

"See you Monday."

"Remember, I'm taking two weeks off to do some work around the house," Bonnie reminded her friend. "Gardening, painting, relining my shelves. And I hope to take in a movie or three. There's a new romantic comedy I'm dying to see."

"Oh, yeah. Sounds like a thrill a minute. Have fun living in fantasyland." Paige locked her desk, flung her purse over her shoulder, and headed for the door. "Join us at the *Fast Lane* if you change your mind."

Was she really so dull? Bonnie wondered as she watched Paige leave. Did she really dress frumpy? She glanced down at her baggy flower print dress and winced. Okay, so she wasn't a glamour puss. But she loathed attracting attention to herself.

She was a background sort of person, taking satisfaction in doing her job well, a homebody who felt more comfortable as part of a group rather than a leader. She preferred pastels to vibrant colors, easy listening to rap, and home cooking over gourmet cuisine.

Unlike her flashy "twin," Elizabeth Destiny, she did not crave the limelight. In fact, she shunned attention. No, Bonnie's number one goal in life was to have a husband and children of her own. But would she ever achieve her heart's desire?

"Not if I have to wear skimpy clothes and hang out in bars like Paige," Bonnie mumbled to herself. Whoever fell in love with her would have to love her for who she was, not for some persona she'd perfected. She'd rather be alone than with the wrong person.

By five thirty, Bonnie had finished her work. Everyone else in the office had long since taken off. Extracting her carryall from her bottom desk drawer, she got to her feet.

Too bad about Elizabeth Destiny and her fiancé. If she were Elizabeth, she'd do everything in her power to hold on to *her* man. Especially a man as sexy and masculine as Kurt McNally. Not to mention good-hearted. McNally was involved in several charities including building houses for the homeless and organizing fundraisers for breast cancer research. From what she'd read about him, Kurt McNally seemed the long-haul type of guy who believed in family and commitment.

So what had gone wrong with their engagement?

Maybe Paige was right. Maybe she did care too much about the lives of celebrities.

Still fretting, Bonnie took the elevator to the first floor and left the downtown San Antonio office building where she worked as a legal secretary. Nibbling on her bottom lip, she joined the thinning crowd on the sidewalk.

The wind gusted, twirling dirt and litter into the air. Scaffolding erected to repair damage from recent hailstorms lined the sidewalk outside the Federal Building.

Traveling beneath the plywood-and-wrought-iron skeleton unnerved Bonnie. She hurried through the makeshift tunnel, head down, her high heels clacking an eerie echo against the wooden walkway.

A construction worker whistled at her, and Bonnie blushed. She wished she was bold enough to flip the guy off, but that just wasn't her style.

Maybe Paige was right; maybe she should start acting more like Elizabeth Destiny. At that thought, Bonnie reached up and plucked the barrette from her hair. Shaking her head, she allowed her curls to tumble free around her shoulders.

"Yeah, baby!" the construction worker hooted. "If you got it, flaunt it."

Bonnie scurried along. Okay, it might be degrading to be objectified, and usually, she would find it offensive, but with the mood she was in, she felt buoyed by the stranger's approval.

She took off her glasses and slipped them into her purse. Maybe she should look into eye surgery, or at least contacts. After all, she was Elizabeth Destiny's duplicate. What would it be like to live a movie star life?

The wind blew harder. Overhead, a board creaked ominously, but wrapped in her thoughts, Bonnie barely noticed.

She reached the cross street and started to step from beneath the scaffolding.

"Lady, watch out!" the construction worker yelled.

But it was too late.

Squinting, Bonnie looked up and saw a heavy two-by-four hanging precariously from a scaffolding beam by one lone nail.

Oh my gosh! The words formed in her mind but froze on her lips.

"Lady, move it!"

Before Bonnie could leap to safety, a single wind puff sent the board flying free from the chassis to hit her squarely on top of the head.

"How you feelin', Boss?"

"I've been better." Kurt McNally ran a hand through his hair and frowned. "Don't those damned reporters have anything better to do than vulture around my ranch? Could you hire security to run them off?"

"I already texted Sheriff Forrester to see if any of his deputies are interested in moonlighting. Might as well keep the money local."

"You're on the ball as always, Hub." He closed the curtains to the bay window overlooking the front yard. Numerous reporters milled near his porch, cameras and boom microphones hovering at the ready.

Hub Threadgill, the ranch manager and Kurt's best friend since grade school, shook his head. At six foot six and weighing less than two hundred pounds, Hub was the archetypal "long tall Texan." Because of his down-home witticisms and prolonged drawl, many people underestimated him, but few made that mistake twice.

"That's what happens when you get mixed up with conniving actresses," Hub said philosophically.

"Rubbing salt in my wounds, Hub?"

"I'm not one to say I told you so but"—his friend shrugged—"I warned you Elizabeth Destiny was a schemer."

"She hurt me bad," Kurt admitted, his voice cracking. Heartache formed a cold stone in his stomach. If it had been anyone but Hub standing in the room, only prolonged physical torture could have wrest those words from Kurt's lips.

"I know, Boss." Hub shifted his weight and stared down at

the hand-scraped hardwood floor beneath his worn cowboy boots. Hub seemed as uncomfortable hearing his confession as Kurt was announcing it, but dammit, sometimes a man just had to get things off his chest.

"I really loved her," Kurt whispered, "or at least I thought I did."

"She's an actress." Hub, apparently not knowing what else to do, affectionately punched Kurt on the upper arm. "She had everyone bamboozled."

"Not you."

"Well, that's only because I been through one exactly like her. You remember Lucinda, don't ya?"

Kurt nodded. Lucinda was Hub's first wife and infamous for her cheating ways.

"Yeah, pardner." Hub tucked his thumbs through his belt loops. "Been there, done that. And it's about as much fun as getting kicked in the teeth by a mule."

"I think the mule would've been kinder."

"Probably," Hub conceded.

Kurt trusted Hub implicitly. They'd grown up together in an El Paso orphanage where Hub's daddy and mama had been dorm parents and Kurt, an abandoned ten-year-old.

If it hadn't been for Hub and the Threadgills, Kurt might have ended up a resident of the State Penitentiary at Huntsville instead of a financial wizard with a penchant for using his money to better the community.

He enjoyed sharing with those less fortunate. Kurt's only self-indulgence was this ranch outside Rascal, Texas where he could escape the rat race and raise prize-winning PBR bulls.

The ranch was his refuge. Eventually, he wanted to settle down here, get married, and raise a family. Mistakenly, he'd thought when he met Elizabeth at that political fundraiser where he'd been lobbying for changes in the foster care system, that he'd been close to achieving his goals.

Elizabeth.

The memory of her betrayal ate at him like battery acid burning through sheet metal. One look in those blue eyes of hers and he'd been a goner, never guessing at the stony soul that lay beneath her warm facade.

Kurt heaved a heavy sigh then blew out his breath in one swift swoop. Yes, Elizabeth Destiny had taught him a powerful lesson about letting his heart rule his head.

Never again.

"Why don't those reporters follow *her* around," Kurt growled, pacing the confines of his office located at the back of the ranch house. "She's the star, not me."

"Boss, you *were* featured in *Texas Today* magazine as one of the most eligible bachelors in these United States. You're a billionaire for crying out loud. You're a hot commodity," Hub reminded him. "Know how many fickle, airheaded actresses it takes to equal *one* of you?"

Kurt snorted and shot his friend a scathing glance.

"Actually," Hub continued, "I was thinking you might turn this fiasco into something of value. Use the press to your advantage. Let everybody know about your pet projects—the houses for the needy you're building with Habitat for Humanity, the walkathon for breast cancer research that you've championed, the changes in foster care you've been lobbying for. Great PR stuff."

"Okay, I get the point; you don't have to sing my praises." Kurt shifted uncomfortably. He didn't do any of that stuff for a pat on the head. He'd been in foster care. He just wanted to help right the wrongs that had happened to him. He was no hero.

"And if you want to be vindictive, you could always tell the truth about your breakup with Elizabeth. I still say it was way too nice of you to let her claim the split was her decision."

"Maybe so," Kurt mused, "but what else was I supposed to do? I'm not the sort of guy who airs his dirty laundry."

"I know."

"It's better this way. Let the engagement die a quick death."

The words were easy to say but harder to live with. For the first time in his life, Kurt McNally had fallen deeply in love, but he'd found out too late he'd only loved an image. Elizabeth had played her part too well, and in the end, she had shattered Kurt's faith in women and his own judgment.

Kurt walked to the window, lifted the curtain again, spied the growing throng of reporters, and groaned.

"Sooner or later, you're gonna have to face 'em. You won't be able to live a normal life till you do," Hub said.

"I know." Kurt sighed. "Might as well get this over with." Putting on his toughest expression, he headed for the door and the bloodthirsty pack circling his house.

2

"Hold on, lady, I called an ambulance."

Groaning, Bonnie opened her eyes. Her vision blurred.

A man's concerned face leaned over her. Who was he?

Better yet, who was she? She couldn't think. Her head throbbed relentlessly. She tried to sit up, but nausea flooded her. Her dress bunched around her thighs. The hard cement felt cool against her bare legs.

"Don't move," the man admonished, slipping an arm around her shoulder. "You've been hurt."

"What happened?" she whispered, lifting a tentative hand to her temple. She gasped when her fingers came away dark with sticky blood.

"A board fell loose from the scaffolding. You took a bad hit. You've been out almost five minutes."

Strangers ringed around her, keeping a respectful distance. Confused, dazed, Bonnie couldn't seem to focus her thoughts or remember where she was going or what she had been doing. Nothing looked familiar.

In the distance, she heard a siren wail.

"Hang on, the ambulance is coming."

"Thank you." Her body floated, limp and fluid.

"I don't mind telling you, you scared me half to death," the burly construction worker in a reflective jacket said.

Bonnie pushed aside his restraining hand and struggled to sit up. Her head swirled, and she swallowed back the bitter taste rising in her throat. Panic tightened her chest. She felt like an inexperienced traveler in a foreign land, lost and unable to speak the language. Her temple hurt, and she still couldn't collect her thoughts. Her stomach squeezed like a vise grip.

"Steady," the guy cautioned.

"Where's my tote bag?" Bonnie asked, grimacing at the sudden pain shooting down her neck.

"Dunno." The construction worker glanced at the crowd. "Did anybody see her bag?"

"Some punk kid took off with it," a bystander said.

Damn, she needed her purse. She'd forgotten her name and was hoping to find something in it that would tell her who she was.

"Lady, why dontcha lay back down, you don't look so good."

"No, please, don't you see? I must have my purse."

"Your purse is gone. Maybe the cops can get it back."

"I must have it!"

"Don't get hysterical. Were you carrying a lot of money?"

"You still don't understand."

"Calm down." He took her hand. "Look, the ambulance is here."

"Ma'am." A paramedic knelt on the sidewalk beside her. "Can you tell me what day it is?"

"Day?" Bonnie repeated.

He nodded, as patient as if he were speaking to a child. "Yes, ma'am, do you know what day of the week it is?"

Bonnie stared at him, dumbfounded. Her gaze fixed on his pencil-thin mustache. "No," she whimpered.

A murmur of sympathy rippled through the crowd.

"Do you know where we're at?"

Bonnie arched her eyebrows. Had the inside of her brain been washed with mud? If she could just squeegee the confusion from her mind, everything would be okay.

"Do you know what city we're in?"

"I'm sorry," she said quietly. A large tear rolled down her cheek. "I don't know that either."

"That's okay. You've suffered a blow to the head. Sometimes it's common to forget things. Now, me and Ralph here are going to help you onto the stretcher...miss, er...what's your name?"

Bonnie searched the group of people standing around her; desperate for some clue, she scrutinized each face. Did anyone know her?

"Oh my goodness," a lady in the crowd spoke out loud and clear. "She's that actress. You know the one. Elizabeth Destiny!"

"SHE'S NOT MY FIANCÉE," KURT MCNALLY GROWLED INTO the phone.

"And good riddance," Hub observed from his place on the sofa, the back of his head cupped in his palms.

Kurt frowned at his friend and waved a hand for silence.

"Ms. Destiny requested that I call you," the doctor on the other end of the line admonished, disapproval evident in her clipped tone.

"Look, I don't care if she *is* asking for me," Kurt said. Let that judgmental doctor try putting up with the likes of Elizabeth Destiny. As soon as Elizabeth pulled her Dr. Jekyll and

Mr. Hyde routine, the doctor would swiftly change her tune. "I've had it with her. You got that? If she wants someone to run to her side, have her call Grant Lewis."

"Sir, your fiancée has suffered a severe blow to the head."

"She's no longer my fiancée," he ground out through clenched teeth. No telling what kind of act Elizabeth was putting on for the doctor.

"She's all alone and begging for you."

Kurt's shoulders slumped. He felt sorry for Elizabeth, and he didn't want to see her hurt. Dammit, after what she'd put him through, how could he still care about her? He couldn't seem to get it through his thick skull that the sweet, innocent Elizabeth he'd fallen so in love with had been nothing but a pretense, a role she'd played to ensnare him.

"What do you want from me? To pay her hospital bills? Elizabeth has her own money."

"Your fiancée," the doctor said, her voice deep-freeze chilly, "is suffering from amnesia brought on by the accident. The only thing she remembered was your name and her own. That tells me you mean a great deal to her, Mr. McNally, whether you like it or not."

That statement stopped Kurt before he could fire off another smart retort. Could it be true? Did Elizabeth care for him on a subconscious level?

"She doesn't want to see me," he denied gruffly, recalling that the last time he'd seen his fiancée, she'd ridiculed him for being gullible and trusting.

"I believe she does."

"Why?"

"She's terrified. Mr. McNally, your fiancée cannot even tell me what day of the week it is."

"Ex-fiancée." Kurt corrected the doctor firmly. He refused to let Elizabeth suck him in again. No way. No how.

"She needs someone here. We're going to keep her

LORI WILDE

overnight for observation, but then we'll have to send her home. She'll need a lot of attention and someone to reacquaint her with the past."

Reliving old times with Elizabeth? Kurt shuddered. Why would he voluntarily relive that torture?

"Elizabeth has no immediate family, but I'm sorry, I just can't help you. I'll give you the name of her agent. Let Howie come babysit the brat."

"I must tell you, Mr. McNally, I find your attitude frankly appalling. Whatever differences you might have with Ms. Destiny, you owe her the common courtesy of helping her regain her memory."

"Doctor," Kurt growled. He'd washed his hands of the woman and good riddance. "Elizabeth Destiny did not know who the hell she was long before she ever got hit on the head. This is some prank she's pulling to jerk my strings, trying to manipulate me into taking her back. Well, you can tell her I'm through playing the fool. She made her choice when she decided to crawl into bed with my business partner."

"I assure you, Mr. McNally, Ms. Destiny's injuries are neither a joke nor a put-on. I've examined her thoroughly. She is suffering from traumatic amnesia, and she may never get her memory back. Now, Mr. McNally, are you going to come be with your fiancée? Or do I have to tell the reporters outside her door that you've refused to see her?"

"Kick me in the keester, Hub."

"Can't," Hub said, his long legs cramped in the passenger seat of Kurt's souped-up Jeep. "You're driving. But I'll make it priority one as soon as we stop."

"Thank you." Kurt gripped the steering wheel and drove around the hospital parking lot, searching for a space.

"I still don't believe you're doing this."

"Me, either," he replied grimly. "Paint me red and call me 'sucker' but I'm a soft touch for someone in trouble, even if that someone is Elizabeth Destiny. Thanks for coming along as moral support. I definitely don't want to be alone with her."

"Can't say as I blame you."

"You think I'm ten kinds of fool, don't you?"

"Naw." Hub paused for effect. "Twenty."

"At least I let her sweat it out till this morning. Made her wonder whether I was coming or not."

"She's still playing you like a puppet," Hub observed.

Kurt smiled. That's what he liked about Hub. No matter what might be happening, the man remained utterly unruffled by external circumstances.

"If I find out this is another one of Elizabeth's publicity stunts..." Kurt let the thought trail off, his jaw tightening at the possibility. The doctor had been very convinced her amnesia was real, but Kurt had seen Elizabeth play countless roles to perfection. She hadn't earned an Academy Award for nothing.

"Boss, you're grinding your teeth."

"Oh, yeah. Sorry."

"Good thing you broke that engagement, otherwise your teeth would be worn to nubs by the time you hit forty."

Kurt slid the Jeep into a parking space and cut the engine. Casting a sideways look at his friend, he sighed, "I thought I'd never have to see her again, Hub."

"Life has a way of sacking you for a loss," Hub observed, "but you gotta keep taking the snaps."

"Thanks for dispensing football homilies, but I haven't run for a touchdown since college."

"I know, just reminding you of your potential to bounce back."

"You're right." Kurt unsnapped his seat belt. "She already ate my heart. What more can one scrawny actress do?"

⁂

THE MINUTE THE MAN STALKED INTO HER HOSPITAL ROOM, Bonnie knew she'd found what she'd been searching a lifetime for.

One look at him confirmed her deepest longings.

This was her soul mate. Her better half. The yang to her yin. For a breathless moment, she felt as if she'd come home, but the angry gleam in Kurt's eyes was anything but welcoming.

She was propped up in bed, surrounded by pillows, and it was a darn good thing because her heart skipped erratically, and her body was flooded by a sudden, intense warmth. If she'd been standing, she'd have passed out cold.

Bonnie knew him with absolute certainty, even though she could not recall her own name without prompting. His every feature was familiar from his tousled tawny hair to his tanned skin to those wide, full lips that hinted at mind-blowing kisses.

He was a big guy, well over six feet, and he possessed exceptionally broad shoulders and a wide muscular chest to match. Tight-fitting jeans showcased his narrow hips and long legs.

One of the nurses had brought in a gossip magazine with Elizabeth Destiny's face on the cover to help her remember who she was. Bonnie had read through the article in the scandal rag a dozen times, trying hard to reconcile the truth of her life. She studied the startled woman's face on the cover with vague unease. Could this person really be her?

It certainly looked like her. Something didn't feel quite right, but what? On the next page was a photograph of the man now standing in front of her, a dour look marring his handsome features. The caption identified him as Kurt McNally. Her former fiancé.

This, then, was Kurt.

Bonnie swallowed, an aching sadness tripping through her heart. It hurt so much not to know what had happened between them. Why had she broken their engagement? Or had Kurt been the one to end the relationship?

For the life of her, she couldn't imagine anyone giving up a man like Kurt McNally. The dull pressure inside her head intensified as she tried unsuccessfully to concentrate.

Despite his imposing size, McNally moved with the fluid grace of a predatory cat—wary, agile, swift.

Bonnie gulped, her eyes tracking his progress as he circled her bed. She was so absorbed by him, she barely noticed the tower of a man trailing behind him.

"Hello," she spoke to the other man. "Do I know you?"

"Yep, you know me. I'm Hub Threadgill."

"Hub Threadgill." She tried the name on her tongue, but it evoked no response in her subconscious. As far as she knew, she'd never seen him before in her life. "I'm sorry, but I don't remember you, Hub."

"That's a pretty tale, Elizabeth," Hub replied, seating himself in a chair at the foot of her bed. He frowned at her and crossed his arms over his chest.

"Somehow Elizabeth sounds so formal. Maybe you could call me Beth."

"Oh, this is rich. I have to hand it to you, lady, you *are* good," Kurt snapped.

"What?" Bonnie's eyes widened. Why did he have such animosity toward her? Obviously, she had a lot of wrongs to right if she hoped to salvage her relationship with him. "What do you mean?"

Kurt clasped his hands behind his back, his shoulders

tense. He cast a sidelong glance at her before taking a deep breath and marching over to her bedside.

"I know what you're up to, Elizabeth, and it won't work, so cut the amnesia sideshow."

Bonnie blinked. The wall of tears that had been building inside her ever since she regained consciousness threatened to burst forth in an unstoppable torrent. She felt lost, lonely, and scared to death.

"I'm not pretending," she said.

"Yeah, right, and the pope's not Catholic."

Her bottom lip trembled. "You don't have to be so mean."

Kurt stared at her. The veins on his neck stood out, his face flushed. "Me? Mean? Turnabout is fair play, sweet cheeks. You play fast and loose with a man's affections, and it's gonna blow up in your face."

A miserable sensation simmered inside her. Kurt *hated* her. What on earth had she done to deserve his vehement loathing?

"I really can't remember anything," she said. "Whenever I try to think, my brain gets fuzzy. If it weren't for this." She thumped the gossip magazine with her hand. "I wouldn't even know my own identity."

"Are you trying to tell me you don't remember *anything*?"

Bonnie nodded. "My mind is a complete blank."

3

Kurt ran a hand along his jaw and narrowed his eyes as he scrutinized his ex-fiancée.

Something wasn't quite right. She *did* seem different. It was more than the white bandage turbaned around her blond head. Her body was fuller, rounder than when he'd last seen her six weeks ago and if possible, she was even more attractive.

For once, she wore no makeup. Kurt found himself approving of her softer, more natural appearance, and that galled him straight to the bone.

Wait a minute, McNally, a voice in the back of his mind warned. This is Elizabeth Destiny. Keep up your guard; don't dare succumb to her wily ways again.

"Did you have more plastic surgery?" he asked coldly.

A hand flew to her face. "Plastic surgery?"

"Your nose. It's smaller, thinner." He cocked his head and studied her profile.

"I...I might have," she stammered. "I can't recall. Have I had a lot of plastic surgery?"

"Just a boob job as far as I know." He stared pointedly at her chest.

Alarmed, Bonnie glanced down at her breasts.

Suspicious, Kurt took another step closer. She smelled different, too, like strawberries and cream; a delicious, wholesome scent quite the antithesis to that exotic oriental fragrance she normally preferred. Unbelievable, but his physical attraction to her tugged stronger than ever. To Kurt's abject dismay, he felt a stirring below his belt.

"What's this all about, Elizabeth? A publicity stunt?" He had to hand it to her, she looked completely affronted by his suggestion.

"I don't want publicity," she said, "and would you please call me Beth."

"But you hate being called Beth, don't you remember? You once told me Beth sounded like a milkmaid's name."

"Well, I've changed my mind."

He leaned over the bed and glared at her, long and hard. She lifted her chin and bravely met his stare. For all her faults, Elizabeth Destiny had never been a coward. Strange, he thought, her eyes were bluer than ever and where had she achieved that sprinkling of freckles over the bridge of her nose? Elizabeth had always been a firm believer in sunscreen whenever she ventured outdoors.

"So," he said, "if it's not money you're after, what *do* you want?"

"Why"—she blinked in surprise—"to salvage our engagement of course."

Kurt threw back his head and let out a laugh so chilling, she shivered. "You hear that, Hub?" he hooted. "Elizabeth wants a reconciliation."

"What's so funny?" she demanded, wadding the bedsheets in her fists.

"Boy, that board did whack you, didn't it? Definitely knocked you into last year."

"I don't find that amusing." Bonnie sniffed. Her head hurt like the dickens, and Kurt McNally thought that was funny.

"Let's get something straight right now. Maybe you are suffering from amnesia, maybe not. I don't know. But there is one thing you can take to the bank, Ms. Elizabeth Destiny, and that is the fact that you and I will never, ever reconcile. Is that completely clear?" Kurt shook a finger for emphasis.

Bonnie slid down in the bed, her temple throbbing, her heart heavy. If Kurt didn't take her back, where would she go? What would she do? She remembered nothing, not even where she currently lived. How could she get to her money? She'd lost her purse in the accident and had no clothes other than the simple dress she'd been wearing when the ambulance brought her in.

"Kurt," she whispered, "I'm so scared."

"You?" Kurt snorted. "I don't believe a word of it. Elizabeth Destiny isn't afraid of anything."

"My mind's a complete blank," she said. "I don't know what I did to you, but obviously it was something pretty rotten for you to hate me so intensely."

"Yeah, well, I suppose we did some rotten things to each other."

It was Hub's turn to snort. Kurt whirled around to stare at his friend. "What?"

"Don't go soft on me now, Boss. Why don't you tell her the truth?"

Bonnie's eyes widened. "Yes. I want to know. What happened to our engagement?"

Kurt cleared his throat. He suddenly felt sorry for her. She did look lonely and frightened.

Don't fall for it. She's the consummate actress, his instincts warned. She'll break your heart all over again.

But what if she really did have amnesia and what if, as a result of the accident, Elizabeth was truly repentant? That idea thrilled him because no matter what she'd done, he still cared about her. Oh, to have the kind, understanding woman he had thought he was going to marry.

A KNOCK AT THE OPEN DOOR DREW THEIR ATTENTION TO the gray-haired woman in the hallway. She wore a white lab coat, and a black stethoscope dangled around her neck.

"Hello," she said, stepping into the room and offering her hand to Kurt. "I'm Dr. Freely."

"Kurt McNally."

"I'm glad you finally came to see your fiancée. We were expecting you last night."

"Yes, well, I am a busy man. I can't drop everything and run when I'm beckoned. My ranch is a good three-hour drive from here." Kurt did not appreciate the physician's condescending attitude. Apparently, like everyone who first met Elizabeth, the woman had been charmed.

The doctor inclined her head. "May I speak to you in the corridor, Mr. McNally?"

"I suppose." Jamming his hands into his pockets, Kurt followed her into the hallway.

Once they were out of hearing range, the doctor said, "Your fiancée has suffered trauma, Mr. McNally. She's lost not only her memory but her whole identity as well. Even her purse was stolen by some hoodlum while she was unconscious. Right now, she feels as if she has absolutely nothing."

"Yeah. Tell me another one."

"Let me explain something to you about amnesia," Dr. Freely said; the pained expression on her face telegraphed her irritation. "It can be temporary, it can be permanent, but it is always terrifying to the patient. Your attitude is not helping matters."

"Wait a minute." Kurt interrupted. "There's something *you* don't understand. My ex-fiancée is an actress; she loves role-playing. She'll do anything to get what she wants, including feigning amnesia."

"Mr. McNally, I'm well aware who your fiancée is, but she is not faking this. She's been examined by two neurologists as well as myself."

"And this means..." Kurt raised an eyebrow, jiggling the car keys in his pocket.

"Ms. Destiny is suffering posttraumatic amnesia in which she can remember nothing about her past. The fact she recognized you at all is nothing short of miraculous."

Elizabeth had remembered him. In spite of himself, Kurt felt an odd mixture of sadness and regret.

Dr. Freely continued, "You know, she didn't even remember her own name until we told her who she was. She does not know where she lives nor what she ate for her last meal before the accident, but she has islands of remembering such as knowing that an astronaut is someone who travels in outer space, a bakery is somewhere you buy bread, and swimming pools are for swimming."

"What do you want me to do about it? You're the doctor. Fix her memory."

"You're an intelligent man, Mr. McNally. I'm surprised at such a silly remark. I'll chalk it up to stress."

"Chalk it up to whatever you want, but I'm not assuming responsibility for her."

"And I cannot just *fix* her, Mr. McNally. Brain injury is a very delicate, very tricky thing. What she needs is time to heal and to be surrounded by those she loves."

"Ha! Good luck there. Elizabeth Destiny loves no one but

herself, try surrounding her with mirrors and adoring fans. She'll snap out of it in no time."

"She doesn't love you?" It was hard to miss Dr. Freely's sarcasm.

"Me? You've got to be kidding. She hates my guts."

"Love and hate are twin emotions, Mr. McNally."

"Call her agent, Howie Jerrell. He's used to picking up the pieces and cleaning up after Elizabeth."

"Actually," the doctor said, "we did contact him. He said she fired him last week, and he was relieved to be free."

"There you go." Kurt raised his hands. "She's made her bed..."

"Nevertheless, her brain scan was normal, and I'm dismissing her this morning. There's nothing else we can do for her here. I've recommended a counselor to help her deal with this, but she's going to need so much more. Obviously, you're a caring man. How much would it put you out to let Ms. Destiny stay with you for a few weeks?"

If Dr. Freely only knew!

"My responsibility to her is over. We're no longer engaged."

"Your fiancée's personality may be totally altered. In essence, she's not the same person she once was."

Hallelujah for something! The woman he'd been about to marry was one conniving, cold-blooded, heartless wench. If by becoming "Beth," Elizabeth had turned into a sweet, good-natured individual, then Kurt was all for the metamorphosis. If that was indeed the cause, too bad a two-by-four hadn't smacked her in the head years ago. It could have saved them both a lot of grief.

The doctor leveled him a serious stare. "I'm asking you as a professional, please don't abandon her at this point. Reach back into the past, Mr. McNally, and find the love you once felt for her. Hold onto that spark; use it to help Elizabeth find her way back."

Kurt gulped. Put that way, his continued refusal to help Elizabeth was downright hostile. But the love he'd felt for her hadn't been real. Too late, he'd discovered he was in love with an image, something that didn't exist.

"To tell you the truth, Doctor, I doubt she'll agree to come home with me."

"Why don't you ask her and see?" Dr. Freely asked pointedly.

Damn. The woman had backed him into a corner.

"Mr. McNally?"

"Yeah, okay, I'll ask," Kurt grumbled. "But I won't beg. If she doesn't want to come, then fine."

"Fair enough." Dr. Freely nodded and extended her hand. "You're an honorable man, Mr. McNally."

Yeah, right. "Fool" was the correct word. Kurt shook hands with the doctor, feeling as if he'd just made the second biggest mistake of his life.

WHILE KURT WAS IN THE HALLWAY CONVERSING WITH DR. Freely, Bonnie used the opportunity to reacquaint herself with Hub Threadgill and the past she longed to remember. She gave Hub a dazzling smile, but he didn't return it.

Clearing her throat, she looked him straight in the eyes. "I'm sorry if I've ever done anything to insult you, Mr. Threadgill."

He grunted, resting a booted foot against his thigh. "You insulted me when you broke Kurt's heart."

Bonnie blushed and lowered her eyelashes. "It's a terrible feeling to lose your memory. My whole history is wiped out.

I'm so sorry about the things I've done, but truthfully, I don't remember any of them."

"How convenient."

"You think I'm faking amnesia, don't you?"

Hub shrugged. "You *are* an actress. I've stood by and watched you sucker Kurt in time after time. I'm here to make sure that never happens again."

"It's not my intention to hurt Kurt."

"Since when?"

Bonnie blinked. "I suppose since I got hit on the head. I'm different now."

"Humph." Hub narrowed his eyes. "I don't know what your scheme is, but you're not getting away with it. Understand?"

"I don't have a scheme." The man offered her no sympathy. Apparently, she had been very cruel to Kurt. She could see the lingering wounds in both men.

"I'm putting you on alert. You mess with my buddy again, and you're messing with me, too. This time I won't sit idly by and let you ruin his life," Hub warned.

Kurt stepped back into the room, and Bonnie's eyes were immediately drawn to him. The man stirred something elemental inside her. She longed to wrap her arms around his strong neck, kiss his full lips, and whisper heartfelt terms of endearment into his ear. And yet, such thoughts frightened her as well.

Bonnie suppressed a groan at the lick of desire building in her lower abdomen. Had he always aroused her this way?

He stood in the doorway a moment, looking at her.

Bonnie shivered under his intense stare.

Arms folded across his chest, Kurt did not smile. His jaw muscles were clenched tight, unyielding. He kept studying her until Bonnie almost begged him to speak his mind.

She sank lower into the bed and tugged the covers up to her neck.

"The doctor is releasing you," Kurt said at last.

"Oh."

"Do you have a place to stay?"

Bonnie shook her head. "I wouldn't even know how to get there if I did."

Kurt made a face. "Um..." He cleared his throat. Bonnie noticed he avoided looking at Hub. "Would you like to come stay at the ranch with us for a few days until you get your bearings and make plans for your future?"

Hub groaned out loud and slapped a palm against his forehead. "What the hell are you doing, Boss?"

"She's got nowhere else to go," Kurt said.

"I ain't gonna be party to this." Hub gritted his teeth.

"Well?" Kurt demanded gruffly, returning his attention to Bonnie. "Are you coming or not?"

"Uh, not if it's going to cause problems between the two of you," she said.

"Ha!" Hub exclaimed. "You thrive on causing trouble, *Ms. Destiny.*"

Hub's animosity cut her to the quick. Had she really been such a horrid person? Perhaps the accident was God's way of giving her a second chance to right past wrongs. Did she have a prayer of making amends?

"Look, my offer is to let you recuperate at the ranch. I know you hate Rascal, so if you don't want to come, that's fine. I'll set you up in a hotel and make your travel arrangements back to California."

Oh, no! Kurt couldn't abandon her like that. He was the only one she trusted. The thought of being trundled off on a plane to California among people she didn't remember terrified Bonnie. Especially if she'd been as nasty to everyone else as she apparently had been to Kurt and Hub.

"My purse was stolen. I've lost everything. My driver's license, my phone. Please," she said, "I'd love to go to the ranch with you."

"So you remember the ranch, do you?" Hub jumped in.

"No. Not at all." Bonnie moistened her lips.

"I think you're lying." Hub narrowed his eyes to slits.

"Stop it, Hub," Kurt interrupted. "This isn't the time nor the place."

"The hell it's not. I can't believe you're dragging her back to the ranch after everything she's put you through."

"She's different now, Hub. Can't you see that?"

"Dammit, Boss, you're one stupid hombre. How much pain you gonna take from this one?" Hub glared and jerked a thumb at Bonnie. "She's an actress for heaven's sake."

"Hub, it's my decision. Dr. Freely says her amnesia is real."

"And you actually buy that?"

Bonnie watched Kurt turn his back on his friend and step closer to her bed. He stared down at her, his dark eyes glimmering with a mixture of hope and hurt. Her heart thudded as if she'd raced the hundred-yard dash in ten seconds.

"Things between us are over for good, Elizabeth; don't you doubt it for a minute. But I will help you until you're well enough to take care of yourself."

"Thank you," she said quietly. "I appreciate it."

"Get dressed. Hub and I will go check you out of the hospital."

She watched Kurt and Hub leave with a heavy heart. A shroud of guilt descended upon her, smothering her with shame. Bonnie threw back the covers and swung her legs over the side of the bed. Her head ached, and she felt more than a little wobbly. Taking a deep breath, she sat there a moment, assessing what she'd learned about herself this morning.

She was not a nice person.

Despite the innocent look on her face in the gossip magazine, despite the glowing words written about her acting talent, despite the references to her great beauty, she, Elizabeth Destiny, was a miserable human being. The negative reaction of those nearest and dearest to her told her that much.

A timid knock sounded at her door.

"Come in?"

The door swung open to reveal a young nurse with a copy of the gossip magazine in one hand, a pen in the other.

"Miss Destiny?" the girl whispered, darting a furtive glance over her shoulder.

"Yes?"

"I know I'm not supposed to ask," the young woman said, "but I was wondering if I could have your autograph.".

Bonnie swayed slightly. The nurse wanted her signature. "Yes, sure, my pleasure." She smiled.

An expression of pure joy crossed the young woman's face. "Oh, thank you." She extended the magazine and pen to Bonnie.

Quickly scrawling the name Elizabeth Destiny under her photograph, she handed the items back to the nurse.

"Wow, Elizabeth Destiny's signature. This is so great." The young woman sighed, looking star-struck. "My boyfriend isn't going to believe this. He's your number one fan. We both particularly loved you in *Some Can Love*."

"I'm glad you enjoy my films."

"Thanks a million."

"You're welcome."

The nurse hesitated.

"Is there something else?" Bonnie asked.

"Uh...well...it's really none of my business," she said, "but I was wondering what went wrong with your engagement? I mean Kurt McNally, whew, what a hunk of man. I can't believe you guys are splitting up."

"To tell you the truth..." Bonnie squinted to read the nurse's name tag, "Tina, I really can't remember."

"Oh, yeah." Tina giggled. "That's right. You've got amnesia. Take my advice, Miss Destiny, and win back that man of yours. There are a thousand ladies waiting in line just dying to take your place."

"I'm sure," Bonnie said dryly. "Now if you'll excuse me, I need to get dressed."

"Oh, yeah. Thanks again." Tina waved, blissfully clutching the autographed magazine to her chest, and closed the door behind her.

Trembling, Bonnie moved to the bathroom to change from the hospital gown back into her rumpled dress. She stared at herself in the small mirror mounted over the sink, searching for answers.

Why was she so hateful? What motivated her? Had she been so hurt in the past that she used cruelty as a defense mechanism?

"Maybe you're just rotten," she whispered to her reflection. "But you've been given a second chance. The slate is wiped clean. You can start fresh. Absolve your sins."

She had a lot of wrongs to right. It was time she made amends for an infamous past she couldn't even remember.

One way or another, she was determined to unearth the truth about her relationship with Kurt. And maybe, just maybe, she could earn his forgiveness.

But first, she had to find out exactly who in the world she really was.

4

The three-hour ride to the ranch was incredibly uncomfortable, both physically and emotionally. By the time they left San Antonio, headed for the Trans-Pecos and Rascal, Texas, Bonnie's head thudded fiercely.

Squinting at the road signs, she wondered if she normally wore glasses or if the blow to her head was responsible for her blurry vision.

She sat in the passenger seat beside Kurt, and Hub had folded himself into the back. They'd driven thirty miles in absolute silence before Kurt and Hub started talking back and forth about the ranch. Not once did they engage her in conversation, both of them acting as if she did not exist.

Swallowing back her loneliness, Bonnie looked out the window as a single tear trickled down her cheek. She swiped it away with the back of her hand, feeling inordinately sorry for herself. She supposed, somehow, she must deserve their blatant disregard.

"Do you remember the lake, Elizabeth?" Kurt asked

gruffly, pointing to a small body of water, surrounded by weeping willow trees, shimmering in the distance.

"No," Bonnie replied, shaking her head. Nothing looked familiar. Casting a furtive glance at Kurt, she saw his jaw tense.

"It's where I asked you to marry me."

"Oh."

"When you said yes, it was the happiest day of my life. Guess you thought I was a pretty big dupe, huh?"

Bonnie's eyes widened as she stared at him. How she must have wounded him. "I would never consider you a dupe."

"You really have lost your memory, haven't you?" Kurt threw her a quick glance, but the expression on his face was impossible to decipher.

"Well, of course, why would I lie?"

"Dr. Freely told me, that in essence, you are a completely different person. I'm beginning to believe her."

"I feel there's a lot of things I must make amends for."

"If you're putting on an act." He raised his eyebrows. "I must commend you. It's your best performance to date."

"I'm not acting."

"Then your transformation is truly astounding."

From the back seat, Hub snorted his disbelief.

"Apparently, I've got a lot to prove." Bonnie looked over her shoulder at Hub.

"What happens when her memory returns, Boss?" Hub grunted. "Then it's back to business as usual."

"You don't like me very much, do you?" Bonnie turned to look at Hub.

"What was your first clue?"

"At least I know where I stand with you," Bonnie countered.

Kurt downshifted as the road inclined. Bonnie watched

his broad hand close over the gearshift, the well-defined muscles in his forearm flexing with movement.

A strange thrill raced through her at the sight. To think those strong, masculine arms had once held her in the throes of passion. Bonnie breathed. Would he ever hold her again? Kiss her? Make love to her?

Thinking about making love with Kurt caused a knot of longing to damn her throat. Without even realizing how, Bonnie knew she'd lost something special.

Perhaps forever.

Maybe, maybe, maybe a voice in the back of her mind chanted, *maybe you can get him back, win him over, convince him our breakup was a big mistake*. But how? She didn't even know what had initiated the original rift between them.

They crested the mountain. Below them, nestled among a peach orchard, lay a white Victorian-style farmhouse decorated with powder-blue gingerbread trim. White wooden fencing ran the perimeter. The trees bore magnificent red-orange fruit almost ripe for the picking. Even in the Jeep's confines, the heavenly aroma of peaches scented the air.

Bonnie rolled down her window and took a deep breath. "Oh my," she said. "It smells delicious."

"We'll be harvesting soon," Hub commented, leaning forward in his seat. "The annual Rascal food and wine festival is next Friday."

"May I help with the harvest?" Bonnie asked.

Kurt and Hub exchanged surprised glances.

"Well?" she asked.

"You hate the outdoors," Kurt said.

"And you despise peaches," Hub added.

What sort of person despised peaches and the outdoors? Bonnie couldn't believe what they were saying about her. Had she really changed so much? It was a disquieting idea.

Kurt turned off the gravel road onto the long caliche

driveway. They passed a black SUV parked to the side of the white wrought iron gate. The driver nodded at them.

"Who is that?" she asked.

"Security to keep the papparazzi away. "

Bonnie noticed a swimming pool to the right of the house. A half-dozen horses grazed in a nearby field.

The wind blew in through the open window, tousling her hair. To Bonnie's surprise, a momentary peacefulness settled over her.

Pulling the Jeep to a stop beneath the portico, Kurt glanced over at her.

She felt his gaze on her face as she unbuckled her seat belt, opened the car door, and stood beside the Jeep, waiting expectantly. The wind caught the tail of her dowdy flower print dress and billowed it up around her thighs.

Kurt stared unabashedly at her legs, and a slight smile curved his lips, fueling Bonnie's hope. He still found her attractive.

Hub, muttering that he had work to do, climbed out of the back seat and loped off toward the red barn.

That left them alone.

Together.

Battling uncomfortable sensations, Bonnie studied her shoes.

"Come on," Kurt said, "I'll reacquaint you with the place."

He ushered her up the sidewalk, past the rosebushes in full bloom. She sneaked quick glances at him, trying to gauge his reaction and stood hesitantly on the front stoop, waiting for him to guide her inside.

Kurt opened the door, ushering her inside.

Her gaze swept the foyer, taking in the gilt-edged mirror, the terrazzo flooring, and the large rubber plant flourishing in the light from the stained-glass windows.

Looking up, her eyes met his. What she saw reflected

there had Bonnie's breath catching in her lungs like a kite in tree branches. Disoriented, she couldn't seem to tear her eyes from his wide, sensual mouth. He smelled of soap and sunshine, a clean, honest scent.

Her heart hammered. The inside of her mouth grew parched. Had he always affected her so viscerally?

"I'll give you the grand tour," he said, clearing his throat. "Refamiliarize you with the layout."

His arm grazed hers as he extended a hand for her to precede him down the hallway. The slight, unintentional touch created such happiness deep within Bonnie that she froze.

A heat of color stained her cheeks. Kurt lifted an eyebrow. Was her estranged fiancé feeling the same inexplicable stirrings as she?

"This way," he said, leading her into the den.

The large family room was equipped with a big-screen TV, video games, surround sound system, and overflowing bookshelves. A plush leather sofa lined a paneled wall, and practical indoor-outdoor carpet covered the floor.

From there, they passed down the hallway to the living room. This area was more lavishly decorated than the den. The furniture, straight-backed and expensive, was not designed for family sitting. A cane-bottomed rocking chair sat in one corner, a brass coatrack in another. Skylights fed sun to a plethora of lush potted plants. Blue-and-beige-striped drapes framed the wide bay window.

Bonnie nodded her approval at the light, airy environment.

"Nice room," she said, "very natural."

Kurt shot her a sideways look. "You used to say it was bland and boring."

"I did?"

"You wanted to redecorate with modern art and mono-chromic designs."

"Really?" Bonnie crinkled her nose. The more she heard about her old self, the less she liked the person she'd once been.

"You really don't remember?" Kurt narrowed his eyes, watching her.

"No."

He shook his head. "Let me show you the rest of the house. This way."

"Kurt, is that you?" a female voice called.

"Yes, Consuelo," Kurt replied, pushing through wooden swinging doors into the kitchen area.

The facilities were thoroughly modern, from the new dishwasher to the complicated oven to the huge stainless steel refrigerator. Mounted from the ceiling over a large butcher-block island were numerous glistening copper pots and pans.

Bonnie trailed behind him, curious about the woman who possessed such a lyrical voice. Was Consuelo Kurt's new girl-friend? Her stomach tightened at the thought.

The room smelled gloriously of roasted chicken, fresh green beans, and homemade bread. Bonnie's mouth watered. A dormant memory stirred in her. She remembered chopping vegetables, boiling water, washing dishes. Had she once cooked in this very kitchen?

A dark-haired woman stood at the sink humming an old ballad, an apron around her slim waist, a cup towel clutched in her hand. The smile on her lips died when she saw Bonnie. Her eyes narrowed, and she set down the platter she was drying.

"What is *she* doing here?" The woman asked, jerking her head at Bonnie.

Bonnie thought the comment entirely rude, but then she

didn't remember how she'd treated this woman in the past. Mortified, she said nothing, merely stood behind Kurt and waited for him to speak.

"Consuelo, Elizabeth got hit on the head, and she's suffering from amnesia. She can't remember anything about her past."

Distrust flickered in Consuelo's dark eyes.

"Elizabeth, this is Consuelo, Hub's wife." Kurt waved a hand at the woman. "They run the ranch."

"Hello, Consuelo." Bonnie offered a timid smile.

Consuelo's back stiffened. "Hello," she replied guardedly.

"If I've been rude to you in the past, I want you to know I'm sorry."

One eyebrow shot up on the woman's forehead. She slanted a glance at Kurt. "Is this for real?"

"Yes," Bonnie said firmly. "Unfortunately, I can't remember anything I've done."

"Sounds too handy to me," Consuelo remarked.

The woman treated her the way Hub had, with obvious disdain. Depressed, Bonnie placed a hand to her bandaged temple. Her head ached something fierce, and she wanted nothing more than to lie down and sleep for a week.

Kurt nodded at Consuelo. "I'm going to give Elizabeth the north guest room."

Consuelo shrugged. "Fine with me, but I'm not waiting on her."

"Oh, no," Bonnie interrupted. "I don't expect you to wait on me."

"Since when?"

"Since now. And please call me Beth."

Consuelo looked at Kurt. "She's changed."

Kurt studied her a long moment. "Yes, I believe she has."

Something inside Bonnie thawed a little. Perhaps, if she tried as hard as she could to make amends for her past failings, Kurt might be able to forgive her and they could give their relationship another try. Although she did not remember what their life together had been like, Bonnie wanted to heal any pain she might have caused.

"This way," Kurt said, ushering her out of the kitchen and upstairs to the second story.

"Thanks for refreshing my memory. It's tough not recognizing anything."

Five bedrooms lay in a circle around the stairs. Kurt informed her that one room housed a complete home office. Of the remaining bedrooms, one belonged to Kurt, and the other three were guest bedrooms.

Bonnie stepped over the threshold into a room decorated in green and white. A striped comforter, complete with a lot of throw pillows, rested on the four-poster queen-size bed. An armoire housed a small TV. Beside it sat an upright piano. Bonnie walked over to the window and peered down at the lush grounds below.

"I hated it here?" she asked, wondering how anyone could hate this charming house.

"Yes." Kurt eased down on the edge of the bed. Bonnie was very aware of his intense scrutiny. "You kept wanting me to move to L.A. You said it was too dull here. No nightlife."

Bonnie turned from the window to face him. "I was a regular party girl?"

"That's an understatement."

"That image of me feels so wrong." Bonnie frowned.

Kurt cocked his head and shrugged. "What can I say, it's the truth." He sat with his palms resting on his knees.

"May I ask you a question?" she asked.

"Fire away."

"Suppose I never get my memory back."

"Okay."

She slanted him a glance. How handsome he looked with

his light-brown hair combed back on his forehead and his muscular body encased in a formfitting white T-shirt. His chin was strong and firm, his teeth sparkling white.

"How long are you going to allow me to stay here?"

Kurt stroked his jaw with a forefinger. "I don't know."

"Do you suppose..." She hesitated, her heart lurching into her throat anticipating his answer. More than anything in the world she wanted to resurrect the embers of their cold courtship. "That you and me...that, well, we...you know...might have a chance to repair our relationship."

Kurt froze. His face was an unreadable mask, his shoulders held stiff and straight. "I'm afraid that's out of the question."

"Even if I've changed?"

"It's no good, Elizabeth."

"Beth. Please call me Beth. I like it much better."

He stared at her a moment.

She gulped. "I'm sorry. So sorry for the hurt I've caused."

"So you do remember some things."

"No. I remember nothing of our life together, but it's evident in the way everyone treats me that I must have dished up a lot of misery and for that, I'm deeply sorry."

He leaned closer, the look in his hazel eyes cold. "How can you be truly repentant when you don't recall the crime?"

"You're right. I can't." Bonnie breathed lightly between parted lips, her mind a jumble of emotions.

"You are...different," he said, his eyes raking over her body with unabashed hunger.

At least his physical feelings for her were still alive. That was a start. Maybe if they rekindled the corporal aspect of their relationship, it would lead to repairing the emotional side.

Bonnie dropped her gaze, unable to bear the desire she

saw on his face. She raised the piano lid and ran her fingers along the keys. "Do I play?" she asked him.

"You never have before. The piano belonged to my great-aunt."

She seated herself at the piano and quickly ran through the scales, her hands moving with accomplished ease.

"I thought you were tone-deaf," he said.

She frowned. "I don't remember ever playing the piano. This is too strange." Hopping up from the bench, she folded her hands, confusion marring her features.

"You must feel very frustrated."

"How come I can play the piano? You said I never played before." A deep furrow knitted her forehead.

"Could be some brain injury phenomenon. We'll ask Dr. Freely."

She rubbed her brow with her index finger as if massaging her head would help her think. "I'd hoped coming here would jog my memory, but it hasn't." Her bottom lip trembled.

"Hey," he said, moving across the room toward her. "You've got to give yourself time. Be kind to yourself."

He stopped just inches from her and lowered his head. Bonnie tilted her chin and looked up into his eyes, and for one startled moment, she could have sworn that he was about to kiss her.

5

Five minutes ago he'd doubted her amnesia. But hearing her play the piano, seeing the fear in her eyes, Kurt was almost sure she was not acting.

He settled a comforting arm around her shoulder, and Elizabeth melted pliantly against him. She tilted her face up, gazing at him the way a disaster victim might look at her rescuer.

"I'm so afraid," she whispered.

"Of what?" he asked, enjoying the feel of her body pressed against his far too much.

Old memories came floating back, memories of a time when he still believed in love and happily ever after, long before he realized what sort of person Elizabeth Destiny truly was. But what about now? Today? Who was she?

Don't fall for it, Hub's voice echoed in his head. *Elizabeth Destiny is a sly one.*

But Beth, as she wanted to be called, looked anything but sly. Funny, how she seemed like a Beth now. Soft and round and innocent. Not at all like the hard, angular, cynical Elizabeth. Could amnesia really transform a person?

"I'm scared of not getting my memory back," she whispered, brushing a lock of hair from her face. "But in a way, I'm more frightened that I will."

"I don't understand."

The feel of her body beneath his hands did crazy things to Kurt's libido. He suddenly found himself battling the urge to kiss those sweet pink lips, to bury his face in that cloud of blond hair and inhale her fresh strawberry and cream scent.

"I want to know who I am." She paused, the fear in her eyes growing larger. "But I'm so afraid of what I'll find out."

Ah, there was that. Kurt said nothing. What could he say?

"I'm a terrible person, aren't I?"

She looked so dejected, Kurt tightened his grip on her shoulder. "In the past, you've used people," he said quietly. "But it seems like the accident has changed all that."

"What happens when I remember?"

"I don't know," he answered honestly. His hand snaked out to curl fingers around her upper arm. "But if you're faking this, so help me, Elizabeth, I'll make sure you'll regret it for the rest of your life."

"You think I like this?" she cried. "It's an awful feeling I wouldn't wish on my worst enemy."

"I thought I was your worst enemy," he said, his tone low, gruff, and menacing.

"You're my only friend."

"Remember," he asked, "the first night we slept in this room?"

"No," she whispered hoarsely.

"I do. You're prettier now, though. Softer. Sweeter. You've put on a little weight, and it looks good on you." Despite his better judgment, Kurt wrapped his arm around her waist and pulled her against him.

A gasp escaped her.

His kiss was rough, demanding. His lips pressed firmly to

hers, his tongue demanding entry to her mouth, seeking to punish her for the hurt she'd inflicted. When she squirmed, he held her tighter.

"Is this what you want?" he asked hoarsely. "Is it?"

"No," she cried, pulling away.

He was so conflicted. Part of him wanted to comfort the devastated Beth, and yet, a warier aspect of him remained suspicious. Threading his fingers through her hair, he tipped her head back and kissed her again.

Something was wrong, Kurt thought, his tongue drinking in the taste of her. The feelings she stirred inside him were different than any he'd ever felt before, stronger, more powerful, overwhelming.

Groaning deep in his throat, he closed one hand over her breast. Funny, she tasted different too. Kissing her now, he thought of home-baked bread and vine-ripened tomatoes. A garden of delight.

"Please," she whispered, trembling in his arms. "I...don't..." She gulped. "Stop it, please."

Kurt pulled back, confused by both his own actions and her response. Why had he kissed her?

"Something is happening to me. It's like I've never been kissed before." She backed away from him, her blue eyes as wide as headlights. "I'm so afraid."

"Good," he said gruffly. "I'm glad you're scared."

"Why did you kiss me?" she demanded.

"To test you," he replied, "to see if you're telling the truth."

"Did I pass your test?" Anger flared in her eyes.

He stared at her. "Yeah, I guess you did."

If Elizabeth had been intent on seducing him, Kurt would have known the amnesia stunt was a charade, but instead, she'd acted as timid as a virgin on her wedding night.

But it didn't matter. Even if Elizabeth had changed, things

were over between them, and he had to make that perfectly clear.

"Listen to me carefully, Elizabeth, and listen good. There will be no reconciliation. You betrayed me and shattered my trust. No matter whether you recover your memory or not, there will be no going back. So do us both a favor and put the idea out of your mind forever."

❦

KURT LEFT ELIZABETH'S BEDROOM, HIS MIND WHIRLING AS dark and destructive as a West Texas tornado. His gut was in little better shape. He couldn't have felt worse if he'd eaten a plate of rocks.

He slammed out of the house and down the back steps, his heart leaping in his chest.

Damn the woman. She'd scrambled his brains once again. Just when he thought he was over her, here she was acting like the sweet, kind woman he'd once believed he loved. Except he'd found out the hard way that the woman he'd fallen in love with had been a consummate actress living a part, and he'd been an enormous blockhead to be so easily deceived.

Not again.

Kurt didn't believe the radical changes in his ex-fiancée; the transformation was too dramatic. Some niggling part of him whispered that things weren't what they seemed. The blow to her head was real enough, but something about the new Elizabeth did not ring true.

What game was she playing?

The wily woman might have decided to take advantage of the mishap for her own nefarious purposes, hoodwinking the neurologists into believing she had amnesia.

But why?

Kurt was determined to unearth the answer. Maybe he could trip her up, catch her in a lie and figure out what in the hell she thought she could gain by this deception.

He'd keep a sharp eye on her, analyzing her every nuance, word, and gesture until he got to the bottom of this hoax.

Unfortunately, some secret part of his heart hoped that the alterations were real, that it was possible for Elizabeth to indeed change, that things could be as they were at the beginning of their courtship.

He caught his breath at that thought.

"Stop it, McNally," he growled under his breath. "Don't you dare toy with such ideas."

But back there in the bedroom, Elizabeth clutched in his arms, her soft flesh pliant in his hands, her honeyed strawberries and cream fragrance enveloping him, he'd almost believed anything was possible.

Elizabeth can only love Elizabeth Destiny, don't ever forget that, he reminded himself.

He stopped outside the barn, rested his arm against the open wooden door, and closed his eyes. He swallowed past the lump in his throat as old memories, lost hopes, and broken dreams ran through his head.

At first, Elizabeth had talked excitedly about having children. She'd reassured him that she loved the country and helping him in his humanitarian pursuits seemed to be her number one goal in life. She discussed getting married on the ranch and even going barefoot to the ceremony as a fertile symbol of her intent to become a farmer's wife.

No doubt about it, she'd charmed the pants off of him, promising to put her acting career on hold for a few years while they raised a family. And, Number-One-Fool that he was, he'd believed her.

"Hey, Boss."

Kurt jumped a foot when Hub laid a hand on his shoulder.

"Don't let her do this to you again," Hub warned.

"She's only here until she recovers her memory, Hub. That's all there is to it."

Hub snorted. "Kid yourself if you want, but you ain't jerking my chain. I know you're hoping she's truly changed this time."

"No, I'm not." Kurt pressed a palm to his nape. "Not really."

Hub stroked his long jaw but said nothing.

"Quit looking at me like that."

Shaking his head, Hub stalked back into the barn.

"What?" Kurt demanded, following his oldest friend.

Hub stopped, flicked a pair of gloves from a peg on the wall and tossed them to Kurt. "Get busy helping me and keep your mind off that woman. It's the only thing that's going to save you."

Tugging on the gloves, Kurt had to admit the wisdom of Hub's words. He would work himself into oblivion so that when his head hit the pillow tonight, Elizabeth Destiny would not haunt his dreams.

BONNIE SAT IN THE QUIET, EMPTY ROOM, TEARS SLIPPING down her face. She'd never felt so alone in her entire life. Or at least what she could remember of her life—which granted, wasn't much.

Didn't anyone love her?

She stood and walked to the window. Pushing back the curtain, she stared down at the yard below and watched Kurt walk to the barn.

Her heart contracted at the very sight of him. A wave of affection washed over her so powerfully, she sank to her knees and pressed her nose against the windowpane.

When Kurt had held her in his arms and meshed his lips with hers, she'd felt as if she'd died and flown straight to heaven. But then he'd told her no hope existed that they might repair their relationship.

Misery wrapped her in an ugly fist and squeezed. Hard. Maybe it would be better if she just quietly left the ranch.

But where would she go? She had no money that she knew how to access, no memory, and according to Hub, no friends. Until her amnesia dissipated, she had no choice but to rely on Kurt's patience.

What if you never get your memory back?

Terrified, Bonnie clenched her hands. She didn't know how long she could tolerate living in limbo. Sooner or later, something had to give.

Taking a deep breath, she got to her feet. One thing was certain, feeling sorry for herself only made matters worse. She wasn't going to sit here as if she were a caged princess. No, if she wanted to correct her past sins, she was going to have to get out there and make an effort, prove to everyone that she was repentant.

Wiping the tears from her cheeks, she walked to the oval mirror that was mounted over the oak bureau. She caught her own eye and raised her chin.

"Okay, Elizabeth Destiny, you've been given a second chance. Rebuilding your life is the most challenging role you'll ever tackle. Get busy and convince Kurt you're a completely different woman."

Spurred into action by her pep talk, she slipped out the bedroom door and timidly eased downstairs. From the kitchen, she could hear Consuelo rattling pots and pans.

The housekeeper was an excellent place to start. Bonnie would offer to help her, and maybe Consuelo would open up and talk to her about the past. Painful as that might be, it had to be done. How could she make amends for her transgressions if she didn't know exactly what terrible crimes she'd committed?

Bonnie pushed through the wooden swinging doors and into the kitchen.

Consuelo was humming under her breath as she removed a loaf of homemade bread from the oven.

The homey scent overwhelmed her with a rush of memory. Frowning, Bonnie raised a hand to her head. In her mind's eye, she could see someone wearing Holstein cow oven mitts, taking a similar loaf from the oven. But it hadn't been Consuelo, nor was it in this house. Who? Where? When?

Before she could explore the memory, a shadow fell across her mind. Closing her eyes, Bonnie swayed against the wall.

"Elizabeth? Are you all right?" Consuelo's voice sounded distant.

Bonnie tried to nod, her mouth dry.

"Here, sit down."

She heard the scrape of a chair dragged across the hardwood floor and felt strong hands pushing her down.

"Take a deep breath," Consuelo instructed, squatting beside her. "Put your head between your knees."

Bonnie did as she was told.

"I'll get you a cool cloth."

"Please, don't go to any trouble."

Consuelo said nothing, but got to her feet and crossed to the sink. Bonnie heard the water come on. Slowly, she lifted her head. Consuelo returned and pressed the damp cup towel into her hand.

"Thank you."

Consuelo rested her hands on her hips and surveyed Bonnie with pursed lips. "I can't help thinking that this is another one of your superb acting jobs."

Bonnie shook her head. "It's not."

"I don't trust you."

"I know." Emotion choked Bonnie, and she feared she might burst into tears. Pressing the cool towel to her forehead, she closed her eyes again.

"You hoodwinked us once. Then you betrayed Kurt. You can't treat people like that, Elizabeth, and get away with it."

"I'm telling the truth when I say I honestly don't remember anything about my past."

Consuelo crossed her arms and tapped her chin with the tip of her index finger. "Well, you're certainly not dressed like the Elizabeth Destiny I remember."

"No?"

The housekeeper stared pointedly at Bonnie's dowdy flower print dress. "What happened to your glamorous image?"

"I had this on when I woke up on the sidewalk after the accident." Bonnie fisted her dress hem in one hand. "I don't have anything else to wear."

"Where are your clothes?"

"I don't know."

"Where were you staying before the accident?"

Bonnie shook her head. "I don't know that, either. It's so frustrating."

"Kurt gave away the things you left here," Consuelo said. "He wanted no reminders."

Bonnie lifted a hand to her throat. Consuelo's words stung. "He must really hate me."

"Put yourself in his place. How would you feel if you had found him in bed with one of your costars?"

Wrinkling her forehead, Bonnie tried her best to reconcile herself with this image. She couldn't imagine herself behaving in such a way. "How could I do that, Consuelo? How could I hurt Kurt like that?"

"That's the sixty-four-thousand-dollar question, Elizabeth. Only you know the answer."

"But I don't," Bonnie protested. "You have no idea how horrible it is to lose your memory."

Consuelo leveled her a cold stare. "I still say this is way too convenient."

"I swear to you, I'm not pretending."

"It's going to take a lot of convincing to get me to believe you." The woman turned and twisted off the gas burner under a pan of green beans.

Bonnie got to her feet. "May I help you?"

"Are you sure you're up to it?" There was no mistaking the sarcasm in Consuelo's tone.

"Yes, please. I'd like to be of use."

Consuelo raised an eyebrow. "All right, then you can set the table."

Resting the damp cloth on the counter, Bonnie washed her hands at the sink. "Where are the plates and silverware?" she asked. "I don't recall."

"Why would you? You never lifted a finger around here before."

"Things are going to change. I'm sorry if I acted like a prima donna in the past. That was very selfish of me."

Consuelo's dark eyes narrowed as she assembled the hand mixer to mash the potatoes. "Plates are in the cupboard, flatware is in the second drawer on the left by the refrigerator."

"How many for lunch?"

"Five. Me, you, Kurt, Hub, Jesse."

"Jesse?"

"Our ranch hand. You tried to seduce him once."

Horrified, Bonnie raised a hand to her throat. "Honestly?"

Consuelo shrugged, then added milk and butter to the potatoes and turned on the mixer.

Lambasted by uncomfortable feelings, Bonnie gathered up five plates and set them out on the sturdy table. Her hands trembled as she reminded herself it would take time to unravel the knots of the past and start to repair the damage she'd caused. Winning friends with Consuelo would not be an easy task, but it would be a big first step toward rebuilding her relationship with Kurt.

Bonnie laid flatware and folded paper napkins beside the plates, her head swirling with troubled thoughts.

Hub, Kurt, and a young man that had to be Jesse came trooping in through the back door, bringing with them the smell of freshly mown grass and sunshine.

"How you doin', honey?" Hub wrapped his hands around Consuelo's narrow waist and dropped a kiss on the back of her neck.

Consuelo turned off the mixer and beamed up at Hub. "Hey, big man, you hungry?"

"Starving."

Bonnie sneaked a glance in Kurt's direction. He stood silhouetted in the light spilling in through the screen door, his eyes trained on her.

He looked as exquisite as a Greek god, his tawny hair dipping boyishly in his eyes, his muscled biceps glistening with perspiration. Quickly, Bonnie dropped her gaze. A heated rush charged through her veins, her heart chugging like an old-time locomotive.

A sudden silence descended upon the room. Tension hung as tightly as a newly stretched fence.

"Elizabeth," Consuelo said at last, "would you mind slicing the bread?"

Relieved at the unexpected source of her rescue, Bonnie nodded and scurried across the kitchen, head down.

Kurt's boots echoed against the hardwood floor behind her. Bonnie gasped at his nearness and wondered what it would feel like to have him treat her with the same loving gestures that Hub had just bestowed on his wife.

Stalking past her, Kurt took his turn washing up at the

utility sink in the washroom after Jesse. Catching her bottom lip between her teeth, Bonnie focused her concentration on slicing the bread, the rich aroma rising up to tug at her memory once more.

She had so many questions and not a single answer.

"What's Elizabeth doing back here?" The young ranch hand asked, breaking the silence.

"She's got amnesia, Jesse," Kurt said, drying his hands on a towel.

Just as Hub and Consuelo had, Jesse threw her a wary expression.

Dejected, Bonnie fought back loneliness. Even the ranch hand hated her. Maybe she should leave. What was the point of staying here fighting disapproval and trying hard to redeem herself when no one seemed willing to extend her a second chance?

Raising her head, Bonnie's eyes met Kurt's, and she knew the answer to that question. The somber look mirrored on Kurt's chiseled features cleaved her to the bone. She had to stay, prove to him she'd changed, and salve the pain she'd inflicted. Besides, where else would she go and how would she get there?

"Dinner is ready," Consuelo said matter-of-factly and settled roasted chicken on the table.

Bonnie helped Consuelo finish setting out the meal, then waited for everyone else to find their seats before she slipped into the empty chair directly across from Kurt.

Whenever she glanced at him, her heart tangoed against her rib cage, and her pulse throbbed through her veins in a staccato rhythm. Something about the way his thick, tawny hair flopped across his forehead totally undid her.

No one spoke. Flatware clinked against china, the sounds echoing throughout the large room.

Bonnie raised her head to find every eye trained upon her.

Unnerved, she cleared her throat. "Listen," she said, growing irritated despite herself. "I'm not going to bite anyone. Please, go ahead and talk about your day."

"You're asking a great deal from us, Elizabeth," Kurt said lightly.

Bonnie noticed he'd only been pushing his food around on the plate, eating nothing. She had no appetite, either. Bravely, she laid her fork down and swept her gaze around the table before meeting Kurt's stare head-on. "All I'm asking for is the opportunity to prove myself. Could you all please treat me with the same courtesy you'd offer any other guest at your table?"

Jesse focused on his food. Consuelo wore a detached expression. Hub's brow narrowed in suspicion.

But it was Kurt's reaction Bonnie wanted.

He cleared his throat. "You hurt every one of us in one way or the other, Elizabeth, and now you expect us to act as if it never happened."

"As far as I'm concerned it never did!" Bonnie exclaimed. She couldn't seem to make them understand how desperate she felt.

"Let's get something straight." Kurt planted both palms flat against the tablecloth. "You treated Consuelo like a servant. You called Hub a 'hick' on numerous occasions, and you tried to seduce Jesse."

The warmth drained from Bonnie's face.

The gleam in Kurt's eyes was purely malevolent.

Her whole body trembled; her jaw worked.

"I...I..."

"Yeah, and that was just for starters. You may really have amnesia, and you may truly be repentant, and I promised the doctor I'd take care of you until you got your memory back. But there's no way you can expect us to act as if you haven't cut each and every one of us to the very quick."

❧ 6 ❧

The meal was ruined.

Hub tried his best to salvage things by shifting the conversation to the peach harvest, but nothing could dispel the disheartening atmosphere invading the room.

Kurt almost felt sorry for Elizabeth. She sat hunched over her plate, her petite mouth a tight seam. Was it his imagination or were her lips wider and fuller than before? Maybe she'd gotten them plumped up with filler.

Her blond hair lay draped over her shoulders as if the strands were slender branches of a weeping willow. And her hair was longer, thicker. Extensions? Her locks were a slightly darker color too. She must have added highlights. She was chameleon for sure, able to transform herself into whatever she wanted people to see.

Blinking, she kept her head down, her eyes trained on her plate.

He suppressed an urge to hug her. *Watch it, McNally, she's bamboozled you more than once.*

Forcing himself to swallow a bite of the green beans

picked from Consuelo's garden, he remembered the time when he thought he was falling in love with Elizabeth. He had mistakenly believed she was precisely the kind of woman he'd been looking for all his life—sweet, kind, loving. In the beginning, she'd smiled often and never complained. She'd tirelessly assisted him in his numerous causes, her energy never flagging, and Kurt had been completely captivated.

He'd heard rumors about her, of course. Several of his colleagues and more than a few Hollywood types had warned him not to trust her. They mentioned her tendency to run hot one minute, stone-cold the next.

Not wanting to believe the worst about his fiancée, Kurt had attributed these rumors to jealous gossips.

It took several months before the real Elizabeth emerged, vindictive and ugly. Right after she'd moved to the ranch with him, Elizabeth abandoned the pretenses she'd affected to get his ring on her finger. She quickly grew demanding and sullen, ordering Consuelo to wait on her hand and foot. Whenever Kurt had asked her to accompany him on business trips, she'd pouted, thrown temper tantrums, and constantly griped about boredom and how she missed the Los Angeles club scene.

At first, Kurt had made excuses for the drastic changes. She needed time to adjust. The difference in the environment had placed a great deal of strain on her. She was an artist and, therefore, high-strung; he should expect some emotional ups and downs.

Yet, her behavior only worsened. She started flirting with his employees and coworkers. She had strutted around the house, dressed in skimpy outfits, showing off her finely sculpted body. If Kurt dared suggest she wear something less revealing, she'd pick a fight and accuse him of irrational jealousy.

He couldn't win. Before long, he was living on a battlefield, never really sure when the land mine would detonate. That, most of all, had been the beginning of the end. Up to the age of ten, he'd been raised in an antagonistic household, and Kurt refused to tolerate constant discord in his own relationships.

"May I be excused?" she asked.

"Pardon?"

Elizabeth's voice, sounding small and downtrodden, snapped him back to the present. She'd never asked to be excused from the table before.

"I'm sorry, Consuelo; the food is excellent, but I just can't eat." She placed a hand to her stomach, tears shimmering in her eyes.

Guilt flicked through Kurt at the sight, then he reminded himself she was a superb actress. Tugging at his heartstrings was what she did best. Hardening his jaw as well as his heart, he nodded.

She pushed back from the table, looking timid.

Again, Kurt quelled the tender feelings rising in him. He scanned the drab dress she wore. It was not at all like something the flamboyant Elizabeth would have chosen, but then he reminded himself she might have purposely picked the baggy clothing to enlist his sympathies.

Well, it wasn't going to work. No matter how hard she might try, he absolutely would not allow himself to be tricked.

"I'm going upstairs to lie down." She cast him a pleading glance as if begging for his forgiveness, but Kurt avoided her gaze.

The room breathed a collective sigh the minute the doors swung closed behind her. Her footsteps echoed on the stairs. As soon as she was out of earshot, everyone started talking at once.

"Can you believe her gall?" Hub shook his head.

"I don't trust her." Consuelo raised her chin.

"Do you think she really has amnesia?" Jesse asked.

"Kurt, you're not getting any funny notions, are you?" Hub asked.

Kurt blew out his breath. "Of course not."

"I think she's faking," Consuelo said.

"Three neurologists say she's not. That's the only reason I agreed to let her come here."

Usually, Kurt wouldn't feel obligated to justify himself to his friends, but they'd been through the wringer with him on this one and felt that he owed them an explanation.

"Hey, Boss." Hub raised his palms. "It's your house."

"We just don't want to see you hurt all over again," Consuelo added, her smooth brow wrinkling.

"I'm not hungry, either." The food Kurt had managed to force down sat like slate in his stomach. "I'm going to the orchard."

Without waiting for a reply, Kurt left them to their meal and slipped out the back door. He tried not to think about Elizabeth, but despite his best intentions, the image of her, head down and wounded, stabbed through his heart.

Chump. Fool. Rube. No matter how many names he called himself, he couldn't stop the emotions tumbling through him, more relentless than a violent storm.

What if she'd genuinely changed? What if she never got her memory back? What if...? Argh! Kurt slapped a palm against his forehead. *Think about Grant Lewis; that should cool your jets, McNally.*

Elizabeth had destroyed a great partnership. After he'd caught the two of them in bed together, Grant had never been able to look him in the eyes. Gallantly, Grant had tried to take the blame for the situation, but Kurt knew who had orchestrated the whole thing. The indolent expression on Elizabeth's face had told the real story. She'd had the nerve to insinuate her betrayal was his fault because he'd been spending too much time at the homeless shelter.

Kurt growled under his breath at the memory. Yes! That's what he needed to remember. Elizabeth's callous disregard for his feelings.

Stalking along the fence line, his mood darkened. His boots kicked up dirt, and his neck muscles corded in anger. He shoved his hands deep into his jeans' pockets.

Angus cattle grazed in the field to his left; flies droned lazily in the July heat, and white clouds drifted overhead. The scent of peaches hung in the air as sweet as a lover's kiss.

He squinted against the sun and looked around at the familiar sights and sounds of his ranch. The moonlighting sheriff's deputy Hub had hired was doing a great job of keeping the reporters away. Or maybe something more newsworthy had happened, and they were off to a hotter story. Good riddance. He was happy to have his peace back. He loved this place. The home he loved like nothing else on earth.

From the time he was a small boy, he'd longed to possess his own ranch. Sometimes that thin dream had been the only thing that helped him through each troubled day. He recalled hiding in his bedroom closet, far away from the screaming and fighting. He'd pretended he was riding horses, swimming in a stock tank, and swinging from grapevines. One day, he'd vowed, one day his dream would come true.

And it had.

He stopped and surveyed the orchard. Rows of peach trees loaded with ripe fruit bent gracefully toward the earth. Leaning one arm against a fence post, he told himself that his business, his philanthropic interests, and the ranch were enough for him. Kurt McNally had no use for that chaotic emotion called love. Elizabeth had burned him once, but no more.

He brooded, his lips pressed into a tight line. Usually, he didn't give in to despair, but the events that had brought Elizabeth back into his life had thrown him for a loop. Kneading his forehead, he wondered what he should do next.

A prop plane buzzed in the distance; perspiration dampened his shirt. His gut churned. A soft, muffled noise garnered his attention, and Kurt cocked his head, listening.

A sniffle? A sob?

He scanned the area, seeing nothing out of the ordinary.

A hiccup.

Kurt looked up. A pair of tanned legs dangled from the nearest peach tree. He moved forward, angling his head to peer beneath the sheltering branches.

"Elizabeth?"

"Go away."

"What are you doing in that peach tree?"

"L...l...leave me alone."

Kurt stepped closer.

She had a tissue pressed against her eyes. Her skirt tail was hiked up around her thighs. The white bandage wrapped around her head intensified her vulnerability.

Dumbfounded, he stared. He could never, ever in his wildest dreams imagine the cool, sophisticated Elizabeth Destiny scaling a tree.

"How did you get up there?"

"I climbed." Her tone indicated he was silly for asking.

"Why?"

"I wanted to be alone," she sniffled, her cute little nose red, her eyes swollen. "So go away."

Elizabeth? Wanting to be alone? Even at the beginning of their relationship, when she was pretending to be everything he'd ever wanted in a woman, she'd hated to be alone. Elizabeth was most definitely a people person.

Had the amnesia affected every aspect of her personality?

She seemed different in so many ways. Much more susceptible. And delicate. Had her bone structure always been so small?

Kurt reached up and plucked a peach from the tree. "Want a peach?" he offered. "You didn't eat much."

She shook her head.

He slipped a pocketknife from his jeans and split the red-orange fruit in two and pried out the pit. Stepping next to the tree, he lifted half the peach up to her.

"Why are you being nice to me?" she asked suspiciously.

He shrugged. "Maybe because you surprised me by climbing into that tree."

"What's so unusual about climbing a tree?" She stuffed the tissue into the pocket of her dowdy flower print dress and took the peach half from him.

"You're not the tomboy type, Elizabeth."

"Beth," she said firmly, her long, blond hair trailing over her shoulder, her lips curling around the succulent fruit.

The sight did unexpected things to Kurt. Blood surged through his veins in a white-hot rush. As her teeth closed over the delicious tidbit, an odd lightheadedness washed over him.

"Delicious," she mumbled around a mouthful of peach as juice dripped from her lips.

"Have the other half." He reached up again, and this time their fingers connected, sending shock waves spiraling through him. Was it his imagination, or had the earth shifted?

"Yum."

"I thought you hated peaches."

"Not anymore," she said, finishing off the peach and happily licking her fingers. Most definitely an un-Elizabeth-like gesture. "I adore them."

"You really do have amnesia, don't you?"

She nodded. "I can't remember hardly anything. When I try to force it, my mind feels foggy, and I get a headache."

"Dr. Freely said it could take weeks for your memory to return."

"She also said I might never remember."

"But hopefully you will."

Elizabeth crossed her arms over her chest and shivered. "I'm scared."

"It'll be all right."

"I don't feel like her."

Puzzled, Kurt frowned. "Who?"

"Elizabeth Destiny."

"What do you mean?"

"She doesn't think like I do."

"You're talking about yourself in the third person."

"I can't accurately describe it, but I feel like she is another person."

Oddly enough, Kurt did, too. This sweet-faced Beth was far different from the cold, aloof Elizabeth. Different even than Elizabeth had been at the start of their courtship when she played the part of naive ingenue to the hilt.

This woman exuded a certain innocence that dwelled beyond surface appearance. An artlessness that seemed to bubble from her very soul. He marveled at the contrast. Could such a drastic alteration be possible? He'd have to read up on amnesia and find out.

"Come on, Beth," he said, surprised at how gentle his voice sounded to his own ears. "I'll help you down."

Tree leaves brushed against his cheek as he leaned forward to wrap both hands around her slender waist. The erotic scent of peaches was almost overpowering. Her thin cotton dress whispered beneath his fingers, and he felt her rapid heartbeat vibrating throughout her tiny rib cage.

Their eyes met. Her lips pursed into a startled circle. Crazily, his breath hung in his lungs. Suspended.

"Upsadaisy."

With one fluid motion, he lifted her off the branch and swung her to the ground. A ripping noise tore the air. Elizabeth's eyes widened.

"Oh my gosh." She reached behind her. "My dress!"

"Turn around."

She did as he asked, her dress tail clutched in her hand.

"Let me see the damage."

She let go.

The garment was ripped up the back all the way to her rounded little derriere encased in white cotton panties.

Since when had Elizabeth worn white cotton panties? She was the red silk thong type.

Something about those plain, guileless panties affected Kurt much more profound than any lace garter or satin teddy. He swallowed a groan of desire. Heaven's above, he couldn't fall victim to runaway lust. Because with Elizabeth, that's all this intense physical attraction could be—lust.

She clutched her dress tail again with a tentative hand. "Is it badly torn?"

"Pretty bad. That's the only dress you've got, isn't it?"

Her curls bobbed when she nodded.

Kurt exhaled between clenched teeth. "I gave away the things you left at the ranch. There's nothing here for you to wear."

"Consuelo told me." Her fingers worried the material. "What am I going to do now?"

Running a palm across his mouth, Kurt tried his best to stop thinking about the sight of her firm, tanned flesh, and those cute white cotton panties.

"I know you hate to wear blue jeans..."

"I do?"

Kurt shrugged. "You used to. Anyway, maybe Consuelo will loan you a pair of jeans and a T-shirt. I'll drive you into Rascal so you can buy some clothes."

Elizabeth bit her bottom lip.

"What's wrong?"

"I don't have any money. I was told my purse was stolen while I was unconscious."

"Don't worry. I owe you for giving away your things without your permission."

"Are you sure?"

"Well, I'm not going to let you parade around the ranch in a shredded dress. Of course, you used to wear much skimpier outfits than that."

Elizabeth rubbed the back of her arms as if cold. "I hate what I keep hearing about myself. I have such a hard time believing how I used to be."

"Believe it."

"You'll never know how sorry I am."

"Sorry doesn't fix the pain, Elizabeth."

"I know."

Her face clouded as if she were about to start crying again. Kurt swore under his breath at the current of sympathy rippling through him. If his idiotic fascination for this vastly improved Elizabeth didn't ease up soon, he'd have to find her new lodgings and pronto. He could not, would not, put himself through the torment of loving her again.

"Let's go," he said abruptly and without waiting for her to follow, stalked through the field as fast as he could.

❧ 7 ❧

Bonnie, who was dressed in a pair of Consuelo's faded blue jeans and a sleeveless yellow blouse, sat beside Kurt, her hands clutched in her lap. She hadn't said a word on the short trip into Rascal, his very nearness left her speechless.

What on earth could she say to the man she'd treated so shabbily? Especially when she couldn't recall her dastardly deeds.

She darted a quick look in his direction. His mouth was turned down at the corners. He'd mussed his hair by repeatedly raking his fingers through it. Dried grass clung to his pant legs, and the top two buttons of his shirt were undone, favoring her with a tantalizing view of his firmly muscled chest.

Bonnie gulped and averted her eyes. She had to stop this. He'd made it perfectly clear there was no repairing their relationship. She'd only torture herself by believing a reconciliation was possible.

Kurt pulled his Jeep to a stop outside a small dress shop on the square across the street from the quaint courthouse built sometime in the late 1800s from the look of the architecture.

Bonnie turned her head and squinted, glancing around for anything that looked familiar, but nothing strummed a chord. As far as she was concerned, she'd never set foot in this town before today.

A large banner suspended between the intersection signal lights announced the annual Presidio County Food and Wine Festival taking place the upcoming weekend.

Heat waves shimmered off the asphalt as they got out of the Jeep and headed up the sidewalk. Perspiration plastered her hair to the back of her neck. Silently, Kurt held the door open and waited for her to enter the store. A welcoming blast from a laboring air conditioner greeted them along with the merry tinkle of a small brass bell perched overhead.

Bonnie blinked, her eyes adjusting to the change from bright sunshine to dim fluorescent lighting. The small store possessed the dry, airy aroma of accumulated fabric. Rows of dresses lined the cement walls, while blouses and slacks rode garment carousels parked in the middle of the creaky hardwood floor.

"I know you'd much prefer to be in San Antonio and raid the chic shops," Kurt said, the sarcasm in his voice unmistakable. "But you're going to have to make do with dated, small-town fashion."

"Oh, this is fine!" Bonnie said, lightly fingering a frilly pink sundress.

A cynical sneer lifted his mouth.

"Really it is," she assured him.

"I find that hard to imagine. I remember you once spent ten thousand dollars in an afternoon at Nordstrom."

"Well, I don't remember that," Bonnie snapped. "I'd appreciate it if you'd judge me on my current behavior, not the past."

"Sorry, no can do."

Just when Bonnie was about to retort, a perky salesgirl bounced from the back of the shop. "May I help you, folks?"

"Yeah," Kurt said, hooking a thumb at Bonnie. "She needs a new wardrobe."

"Oh my gosh!" The girl squealed, and her eyes rounded. "You're her. You're him. I mean you're them!"

Unnerved, Bonnie lifted a hand to her throat.

The girl pointed her finger, her compact body wriggling with excitement. "Sarah Jane, come quick! You're not going to believe who's here!"

Kurt shifted his weight, winced, and raised a finger to his lips. "Shh."

But it was too late, Sarah Jane poked her head out of the storage room. "What is it, Tammy?"

"You're gonna die." Tammy sprinted over to grab Sarah Jane by the hand. "Elizabeth Destiny and Kurt McNally are standing in our store!"

"No way," Sarah Jane said.

"Way!" Tammy sang.

"They can't be. They broke up. I saw it on TMZ." Sarah Jane stood on tiptoes to peek over the garment racks at them.

"You believe those gossip shows or your own eyes? I tell you it's them."

"Let's get out of here," Kurt whispered under his breath. "We can try the store on the other side of town." He looped his arm through Bonnie's and tried to drag her out the door, but she dug in her heels.

"Running off would be rude."

Releasing her, Kurt stepped back. "I see some things never change, Elizabeth. Once a publicity hound, always a publicity hound."

Bonnie glared at him. He'd mistaken common courtesy for attention seeking. To heck with him. Apparently, he was determined to believe whatever he wanted, no matter the truth.

"See! I told you." Both Sarah Jane and Tammy were beside them now, jumping up and down like crazed cheerleaders.

Sarah Jane's mouth flopped open. "Can we have your autograph, Miss Destiny?"

Bonnie blushed. "Sure."

Rolling his eyes, Kurt moved away. Lifting her chin, Bonnie decided to ignore him.

"So when did you guys get back together?" Tammy breathed while Sarah Jane went for pen and paper.

"We're not together," Kurt growled.

"Come on, you can't fool us." Tammy's eyes glistened with a romantic sheen.

"It's a secret. Please don't spread it around town," Bonnie said.

"You can count on us," Sarah Jane said, thrusting the writing instruments at Bonnie. "Mum's the word."

Picking up the pen, Bonnie wrote: To Sarah Jane and Tammy, two of the sweetest girls in Rascal, love Elizabeth Destiny.

"Oh my gosh, oh my gosh," Tammy breathed and clutched the paper to her chest.

"We'll frame this one and hang it up in the store. But you've got to do a separate one for each of us," Sarah Jane said.

Smiling, Bonnie complied while Kurt restlessly paced, his teeth clenched.

"Thank you so much." Tammy smiled.

"You're more than welcome." Bonnie beamed. Warm feelings surged through her at the girls' admiration and respect. For the first time since the accident, she felt wanted, honored, and loved. "Could you girls do me a big favor?"

"Anything." Sarah Jane breathed.

LORI WILDE

"Help me pick out some clothes."

Tammy squealed with delight. "You mean it?"

"Sure. I'd love your input."

"Well," Sarah Jane said, "if you want my opinion, Ms. Destiny, you're way too classy for this place."

"Sarah Jane's right." Tammy nodded. "You should be shopping at Neiman or Saks."

"Actually, I'd like to pump money into the local economy. And believe it or not, I'm striving for the country girl look."

"We can definitely do country, can't we, Tammy?"

"Sure. We understand," Sarah Jane replied. "You want something just right for the festival."

Bonnie cast a glance over her shoulder at Kurt. He lounged against the wall, his hands stuck deep in his pockets, his eyes narrowed suspiciously. She flipped her hair and returned her attention to the girls. If he wanted to pout and brood, then so be it. She'd found acceptance in this dusty little store, and she was going to enjoy her notoriety. If that put Kurt McNally's nose out of joint, too bad.

The three of them had a grand time. Bonnie barricaded herself in the dressing room while Tammy and Sarah Jane scurried to and fro, handing her outfits over the door.

"Come model for your sweetie," Tammy said, after thrusting a pale blue denim romper at her.

"Who?" Bonnie asked.

"Kurt, silly," Sarah Jane giggled. "Like all men who go shopping with their ladies, he's out here looking like a torture victim."

Bonnie smiled at Sarah Jane's analogy and wriggled into the romper. It zipped up the front and had tiny red strawberries stitched across the yoke. The garment skimmed her narrow waist and flared over her hips to hit her leg at midthigh. She pushed open the dressing room door and twirled around the shop.

"What do you think?" she asked, stopping in front of Kurt.

His gaze swept her body. Was it her imagination or did his breathing quicken?

"Not your usual style," he replied tersely.

Bonnie rested her hands on her hips. "What's that supposed to mean?"

He shrugged.

"Well, I'm up for something different." She stalked over to the dress rack, surprised at her sudden anger. Did he have to hang on to his grudges with such a death grip?

Plucking the frothy pink sundress from the rack, she held it up to her shoulders. "What do you think about this?"

"Does it matter what I think, Elizabeth?"

"Yes, Kurt, it does. Your opinion is important to me."

"If my opinion is so important, why didn't you ask me before telling those salesgirls we were back together?"

"I didn't tell them. They assumed it. And I did ask them to keep it a secret."

"You should know that in Rascal, the word 'secret' translates into gossip to your heart's content. It'll be all over town by morning."

"You're being silly."

"I suppose you're going to deny this is just a bid for attention."

"Come on, Kurt," Bonnie tried to cajole him. His insinuations cut her deeply. "Don't be that way."

"I'm not falling for your acting again, Elizabeth. Once was plenty."

"Damn it." Bonnie stamped her foot. "Will you stop being so pigheaded? I'm not acting. I really do have amnesia."

"Please remember we have an audience." Kurt inclined his head at Sarah Jane and Tammy whispering in the corner. "Oh, silly me, you love showing off for an audience, don't you?"

"That's mean."

"If the shoe fits..." Frowning, he crossed his arms.

She longed to traverse the short distance between them and touch him. His pain was easy to read; she ached to make amends. But if she reached out to him and he retreated, she didn't think she could bear his rejection. "Please." She held the dress aloft. "Do you like it?"

"It's very frilly. Totally unlike you."

"I'll get it."

"Suit yourself."

"I will."

"You always have. Why stop now?" he mumbled under his breath.

Tears stinging her eyes, Bonnie turned away and hurried over to the cash register. "Please, ring this up," she told Tammy. "Plus the romper, a couple of pairs of jeans, and those blouses I tried on."

Kurt came to stand behind them. Fishing in his wallet for his credit card, he dropped it on the counter then moved back. Tammy chattered gaily, but Bonnie, wrapped up in her own misery, didn't hear her.

"Are you?" Tammy asked.

"Huh?" Bonnie forced herself to look at the cheerful salesgirl.

"Are you guys participating in the Food and Wine Festival?"

"No," Kurt said adamantly.

"Yes," Bonnie spoke at the same time.

"We're just selling peaches." Kurt shook his head.

"Oh, no." Tammy shook her head. "You've got to participate. Wren Winslow, the festival coordinator, is desperate for volunteers. She's especially looking for someone to be in the kissing booths. You'd be a smashing success, Ms. Destiny."

"You could help, too, Mr. McNally." Sarah Jane chimed in. "We need volunteers for the dunking booth as well."

"Sorry, but I don't think so."

"I thought you contributed to humanitarian charities," Sarah Jane chided, wagging a finger at Kurt.

"I'll be happy to make a donation," he said.

"Ah, that's no fun." Tammy pursed her lips and ran his credit card through the machine.

"It's for a good cause," Sarah Jane wheedled. "Restoring the old courthouse. And Elizabeth, the kisses are only on the cheek or forehead."

"Sarah Jane and I are working the kissing booth, too," Tammy added.

Kurt shook his head. "I appreciate the offer, girls, but no."

"I'd be happy to participate," Bonnie announced. "How do I sign up?"

"Elizabeth," Kurt said, his voice sharp-edged with warning.

Bonnie ignored him and smiled at Tammy and Sarah Jane.

"I'll tell Wren." Tammy clapped her hands. "Wow. The Oscar-winning actress, Elizabeth Destiny, manning the kissing booth at the Presidio County Food and Wine Festival. Who would have imagined? We'll make a fortune."

Tammy sacked Bonnie's purchases and handed Kurt his credit card. "Come on, Mr. McNally, smile. It'll be fun. I promise."

He glowered. "Let's go." He grasped Bonnie's elbow and propelled her toward the door.

"What are you trying to pull?" Kurt demanded once they were out on the deserted sidewalk. His nostrils flared, and his eyes hardened into flat beads. His grip on her wrist tightened. Spinning her around, he jutted his jaw in her face. "Volunteering us to work the festival together!"

From her peripheral vision, she spotted Sarah Jane and

Tammy, their faces pressed against the shop window with avid interest.

"Ah, Kurt, don't be such a spoilsport. It sounds like fun."

"You'd think by now you'd have your fill of kissing strangers, but I suppose not."

"That was the old Elizabeth. I'm not responsible for the things she did. I'm 'Beth,' and I'm different. I'm tired of being maligned and made to feel guilty for transgressions I can't remember. You've been nothing but cruel since you picked me up at the hospital. If I'm so damned horrible, how come you agreed to let me stay at the ranch?"

"You want to know the real reason?" he growled.

"Yeah." She settled her hands on her hips and glared at him, the paper sack crackling against her fingers.

"Because your doctor pressured me into it."

"Oh? Are you that easily cowed by the medical profession? If you really hated me as much as you claim, you would have told the doctor to go jump in the lake."

"Okay. I felt sorry for you, Elizabeth. Pity. That's what motivated me to come get you. Pity and nothing else."

"Why would you pity me?"

"Because you have no one. No family. No real friends. All the people that crowd around you are just hangers-on, fans, or admirers who know nothing of the real Elizabeth Destiny. They fall for your consummate acting job just like I did. They're mesmerized by your beauty, and I'll admit, I was fool enough to be attracted to outer appearances. But those of us who know you, me and Hub and Consuelo, Grant and Jesse and Howie, we know you walk all over people and treat them like dirt once they've served their purpose."

"No," she squeaked.

"Yes."

"Is that how you really feel?"

"Absolutely."

"And with the hate, you don't feel any love left between us?"

"None," he said harshly.

"Well, excuse me, I won't be a burden on you any longer." Pivoting on her heels, she stalked away, an avalanche of tears straining at the back of her eyelids.

"Where do you think you're going?" he called out. "You've got no place else to turn."

The hot Texas sun beat down, causing the wound at her temple to throb painfully. Dizziness swept over her. She'd had nothing to eat all day save for the peach Kurt had fed her. Bonnie pressed a hand to her head, swallowing back nausea and shame.

"Elizabeth."

She stumbled over a crack in the sidewalk. He hated her. She dropped her sack and started running, wind rushing past her ears. Kurt truly hated her.

"Elizabeth, come back!"

She heard his footsteps behind her, and she sped up. Parking meters flashed by. Bonnie had no idea where she was running to, knew only she had to escape the past, an ugly past that haunted and taunted her wherever she turned.

Her breath shot out in ragged gasps as she reached the end of the sidewalk and stepped onto the road.

"Watch out!" Kurt cried.

Bonnie turned her head in time to see an old pickup barreling straight for her, a wire pen filled with Leghorn chickens situated in the truck bed. Stupidly she froze, her mouth agape. The look on the driver's face was one of pure surprise.

❧ 8 ❧

A horn blared. Brakes screeched. Feathers drifted in the air.

Kurt slammed into her as if he were a linebacker sacking a quarterback. She flew across the intersection, put out her hands to catch herself, her palms and knees skidding over the asphalt.

She lay on the ground, breathing heavily and staring at the truck tires just inches from her head. She was too frightened to move.

A car door slammed. The angry, excited voice of the pickup driver reached her ears.

"What the hell do you think you were doing, missy!" the elderly farmer in overalls and work boots shouted. "You could have got yourself killed. Didn't you see me comin'?"

"I'm sorry," Bonnie blubbered.

"Are you plumb blind?" the old man ranted, obviously shaken up.

"I...I didn't see you."

"'Cause you weren't payin' attention. If this fella hadn't a pushed you out of the way, you'd be squashed like a melon."

He clapped his work-roughened hands and shook his shaggy gray head.

"Quit shouting at her, can't you see she's upset?" Kurt asked.

"She's upset! I'm the one who almost committed vehicular homicide." The old man paced beside his truck, the disturbed chickens clucking loudly. "I suppose you're gonna be hollerin' about a lawsuit."

"Hush," Kurt told the farmer. Bending low over Bonnie, his strong arms encircled her waist, his sweet masculine scent comforting her.

"Beth? Are you all right?" he whispered.

Bonnie trembled from head to toe. The knees of Consuelo's blue jeans were torn. Her palms, skinned and bloody, stung like the dickens.

Kurt pulled her to her feet, his hands brushing at the dirt and grime clinging to her clothes. He cradled her in the crook of his arm, clicking his tongue at the sight of her hands.

"Is she okay?" the old man asked.

"I'm fine," Bonnie said weakly. "Just scared."

"Me too," the farmer confessed.

"Let's get off the road." Kurt guided her onto the sidewalk. He retrieved her fallen sack of clothing and helped her over to the drugstore on the opposite corner.

Bonnie allowed him to take charge, appreciating his concern. No matter how much he tried to deny it, his actions spoke louder than his words. He did still care about her.

The drugstore's interior was dim and cool and smelled of lemon cough syrup. Overhead, a ceiling fan rotated lazily. A magazine rack, stocked with newspapers and comic books, sat by the front door. From the piped-in stereo system, Jerry Lee Lewis sang "Great Balls of Fire." An old-fashioned soda fountain sprawled at the back of the building.

A memory skittered through Bonnie's consciousness. She

saw an image of herself as a young girl perched on a red vinyl stool in a similar drugstore soda fountain. She wore a pink ruffled pinafore with bowed pigtails trailing down her back. Mentally, she pictured a smiling, plain-faced woman standing behind the counter. The woman served her a grilled cheese sandwich, barbecued potato chips, and a cherry cola.

Aunt June.

Feeling giddy, Bonnie tapped Kurt on the shoulder with her knuckles, her raw palms held upward. "I remembered something."

He stopped in front of the first-aid aisle, her sack of clothing tucked under his arm, and swung his gaze around to assess her.

"What?" he asked warily.

"Something from my childhood. I've been in a drugstore like this one. Many times. My aunt June worked there."

"Aunt June?" Kurt frowned. "You told me you had no family."

"I have an aunt named June," Bonnie insisted. "Or had."

Kurt raised an eyebrow. "Perhaps you lied to me in the past. It wouldn't have been the first time."

Bonnie leaned against the white metal shelf but said nothing.

"What else do you remember?" Kurt picked up a bottle of hydrogen peroxide, paper tape, antibiotic ointment, and a package of gauze bandages.

She shook her head. "That's it." The memory winked out as swiftly as it had appeared.

"I guess it's a start."

They went to the checkout counter. Bonnie stood behind Kurt while he paid, trying hard to recreate the mental image, but her knees and hands throbbed so hard she couldn't think. A few minutes later, they left the store and her brief flash of memory behind.

Once they were back in the Jeep, he tore open the gauze package and uncapped the peroxide. Bonnie wrinkled her nose as Kurt dampened the gauze with antiseptic.

"Give me your hand," he said.

She held out a palm, and he cupped one hand beneath it, the warmth of his skin unsettling her. He dabbed at her abrasions. Bonnie sucked in her breath.

"I must admit," Kurt said, "you scared the fire out of me when you stepped in front of that farmer's truck."

"Thank you for pushing me out of the way."

He lifted his head and met her eyes. "If I hadn't pushed you, you probably wouldn't have gotten skinned up."

Bonnie swallowed hard and stared ruefully at her jeans. "I ruined Consuelo's pants."

"I'll compensate her."

"I already owe you for the new clothes."

"Don't worry about it." After applying the ointment, he wrapped her hand with gauze and taped it into place. "Now the other one."

Obediently, Bonnie lifted her other palm. His touch was gentle, almost a caress. His head was bent studiously, his breath warm against her skin.

The moment was strangely magical. Afternoon sunshine sloped across the dashboard, bathing them in an orange glow. The leather seat felt butter soft beneath her bottom. The gearshift pressed against one leg as she leaned forward. Kurt's tawny hair tumbled across his forehead like a fat question mark.

Bonnie's gaze traversed the contours of his face—his classic nose, his angular cheekbones that hinted at Native American ancestry, his long eyelashes.

A face she loved.

Loved.

With a start, Bonnie realized it was true. No matter how

he felt about her, she loved Kurt McNally. If only she could remember their past together. Was this love for him newfound? Had the blow to her head activated these intense emotions? Or despite her awful behavior, had she always been deeply in love with him?

Kurt tilted his head. His green-gold eyes stared intently, searching, probing, as if seeking the answers to her soul.

Bonnie gulped. His full, tempting mouth was inches from hers. Millimeters actually and if she moved forward just the tiniest bit...

His grip tightened, and her fingers tingled from the intense sensation. The pulse at the base of his neck quickened.

Bonnie's lips parted.

"Elizabeth," he said, his voice scratchy.

"Kurt," she whispered.

The memory of the kiss he'd given her that morning in the bedroom flashed through her mind. How she longed to taste him again, to savor the feel of his warm, moist mouth. That kiss had been hard, demanding. This time, she wanted something soft, submissive, with a hint of tenderness.

She leaned closer, so close she felt the flushed heat radiating from his pores. His cologne's sharpness heightened her olfactory sense. Tentatively, she wet her lips with the tip of her tongue.

Kurt appeared frozen to the seat. She stared into his eyes and tried to read the depths of him. Confusion dilated his pupils. She could tell he wanted to pull away, and yet, he seemed incapable of moving.

Like a delicate butterfly descending lightly upon a sun-ripened rose, Bonnie pressed her mouth to his.

His eyes shuttered closed. The muscle in his jaw spasmed.

She shifted against him. "Oh, Kurt," she sighed.

"Stop this, Elizabeth." Opening his eyes, he released her hand and sat back against the seat.

"Why?" She blinked, struggling to keep the hurt from her face.

"I can't trust you."

She turned her head, easing back over to her side of the vehicle. "Your mind is made up, isn't it?"

"Yes."

❦

BLOWING OUT HIS BREATH, KURT PEERED THROUGH THE windshield, the steering wheel gripped so tightly in his hands his knuckles whitened. The peroxide bottle clutched between his thighs buckled from the pressure and oozed liquid onto the knees of his jeans.

Capping the antiseptic, he tossed it onto the floorboard and keyed the engine.

"You simply can't believe I've changed."

Glancing over his shoulder, he backed out of the parking lot. "I believe you."

She raised her eyebrows. "Then why...?"

"Because, Elizabeth, if I allow myself to get close to you again, sooner or later your memory will return. And along with your memory, I'm sure you'll recover that selfish personality of yours."

"You don't think the accident could change me for good?"

"No." He headed to the ranch.

"I'll never again be that person you remember with so much animosity."

"Forget it, darling, I simply can't take the gamble. Once scorched by the great imposter, Elizabeth Destiny, only a complete fool would crawl back for seconds."

That night, Kurt couldn't fall asleep. He tossed and

turned in his king-size bed, knowing only one thin wall separated him and Elizabeth. For all the bad feelings she stirred in him, he could not stop thinking about her—her fragrant lips, her fruity scent, her feather-soft hair.

Groaning, he turned on his side and curled one knee to his chest. He couldn't believe she'd kissed him.

A sweet, naive kiss that conjured images of home, hearth, and family. The very ideals he'd been searching for his entire life. He'd fallen for that fairy tale once with Elizabeth, duped by her acting abilities. But this time, she was most definitely different.

What happens when her memory returns?

Kurt sighed and rolled over onto his back. The digital clock-radio glowed red. One thirty.

"Go to sleep, McNally," he growled to himself, but when he closed his eyes, Elizabeth's face hovered before him. Her blue eyes wide, her strawberry lips parted, her small nose quivering ever so slightly.

Propping himself up on one elbow, he turned on the radio. The soothing sound of a Mozart aria floated through the room. Settling down into his pillow, he tried to quiet his mind.

Relax. Take a deep breath. That's it.

His eyes closed; he drifted.

Elizabeth.

He remembered the night they met. As corny as it sounded, their first encounter had been like a scene from a romantic movie. That should have been his first clue that their coming together had been carefully orchestrated, not by fate but by Elizabeth Destiny herself. He and Grant Lewis had been invited to a celebrity charity bash at Dallas's West End. The place was noisy and crowded. Kurt had turned around to shake hands with someone when he'd caught sight of Elizabeth.

A dozen adoring men vied for her attention, but in the midst of them, she managed to look completely alone. Her blond hair swirled around her narrow shoulders like a whisper. The designer dress she wore, sequined, red, and strapless, had glittered in the theatrical lighting.

She'd raised her head, and their gazes met. She'd run the tip of her tongue over her lips. Blue and bold, her eyes held his for two seconds, and then she glanced away. But it was too late. Kurt had been snagged—hook, line, and sinker.

Perhaps if he hadn't been less anxious to get married, he would have recognized the feelings as pure physical attraction and nothing more. Unfortunately, he'd met Elizabeth at a vulnerable time in his life.

The truth of the matter was, Elizabeth Destiny had been in the right place at the right time. Or rather, as Hub liked to point out, the wrong place at the wrong time.

Beth.

That's how he thought of her now. Since the accident. Sweet Beth. Exactly the person he'd always wanted Elizabeth to be.

Beth came to him in his dreams, wearing a long, white nightgown. He could see her spectacular figure silhouetted through the gauzy material—her high, firm breasts, the smooth curve of her hips, her long, shapely legs.

He held out his arms, and she came to his bed, cupped his face in her hands and stared intensely into his eyes, wrapping him in a scent as delicious as fresh peaches and cream.

Pulling her down on top of him, he pressed her to his chest and sucking gently, captured her bottom lip between his teeth. She giggled, her nipples jutting hard through her nightgown, the intoxicating fabric scratching a torturously beautiful sensation against his bare skin.

"Beth, Beth, Beth," he breathed. Had he died and flown

to heaven? He must have, how else could he be here in the arms of an angel?

Then suddenly her soft giggles dissolved into a harsh, high-pitched cackle. Beth's face crumpled, shifted, and changed into the cruel, sharp features of a female she-wolf.

Kurt shouted, bolting upright in the bed.

His body was bathed in sweat. His heart hammered. Gulping, he turned on the bedside lamp, one palm splayed across his chest.

The nightmare mirrored his greatest fear—falling in love with Elizabeth again only to find nothing had changed, that beneath the innocent mask of amnesia lurked a soul of stone.

9

C hurch.

She had to get up for church. Bonnie's eyes flew open, and she glanced at the clock. Whew. It was only seven thirty. She hadn't overslept.

Wait a minute.

She sat up, a hand reaching to gingerly massage her head wound. Was this a memory? With absolute certainty, she knew she went to church every Sunday. But for the life of her, she didn't remember which church or where, nor did she recall the denomination. She simply knew she went to church on Sunday mornings.

Bonnie threw back the covers, got out of bed, and stretched, her fingers reaching for the ceiling. A smile lingered on her face. She'd had the most wonderful dream about Kurt. A dream that had her blushing.

Hurrying through her shower, she dressed in strappy pink sandals and the pink sundress she'd purchased from Tammy and Sarah Jane. She plaited her hair in a French braid, then scurried downstairs.

Nervousness washed over her as she pushed open the

swinging doors into the kitchen. Hub, Consuelo, Kurt, and Jesse sat around the breakfast table dressed in their Sunday best. All eyes stared at her.

"Good morning," Bonnie chirped.

Last night, before falling asleep, she'd made the decision to treat them with sincere kindness no matter how they treated her. Sooner or later, she'd win them over, convince them she could be a decent person.

"Morning," they all mumbled, except Kurt.

He stood up, his chair scraping across the floor. His gaze roved over her body. In his gray suit, white shirt, and blue tie, he was incredibly handsome. Bonnie ducked her head and peeped at him sideways.

"You look nice," he said.

"Thank you."

"What are you doing up so early?" he asked, his brows dipping in suspicion. "You usually sleep until noon."

Clearing her throat, she squared her shoulders. "From now on, please don't assume anything about my behavior."

"Oh, no?"

"I'm going to church."

"Church?" His mouth dropped open.

"Church," she said firmly and seated herself at the breakfast table.

"You've never been to church with us before."

"No, no." Bonnie raised a finger. "Accept me for what I am right now. Please."

Kurt shrugged and sat back down.

Consuelo passed Bonnie a fruit plate.

"Thank you." Bonnie smiled at the housekeeper.

"You're welcome," Consuelo replied and returned her smile.

Maybe she was indeed making headway. The conversation resumed, and they finished breakfast. Bonnie helped

Consuelo clean the kitchen while Hub brought his family car around to the back door.

They piled in and headed for Rascal.

A strange sense of excitement swelled inside her. Bonnie smiled. For the first time since the accident, she felt good—both physically and emotionally. She'd removed the bandages from her palms; the abrasions were healing. Her heart filled with affection for the people in the car with her. They were good folks. Leery of her to be sure, and worried she'd hurt them again, but they were willing to give her a second chance. What more could she ask for?

They arrived at the Methodist church. To Bonnie's surprise, Kurt came around and helped her out of the car. He wrapped his hand securely around her elbow as he guided her up the sidewalk behind Hub, Consuelo, and Jesse.

Well-dressed parishioners greeted them. An excited buzz ran through the crowd as people recognized her, and some waved at her. Most simply stared. Kurt put his arm around her shoulder and drew her close. Nothing had ever felt so comforting. At least not that she remembered.

"Please don't embarrass me in front of my friends," he whispered. "And don't tell anyone we're getting back together. You know there's no hope for that."

Then he released her and stepped away.

Her happiness evaporated instantly. Just when she thought Kurt might harbor feelings for her, he'd distanced himself. How could she ever hope to win him back?

Forcing herself to keep smiling, she shook hands with strangers and made small talk until it was time for the services to begin. It appeared most of the townspeople did not know her very well. Many seemed hesitant to approach. Feeling subdued, Bonnie didn't encourage them.

They filed into the church, and Bonnie seated herself in the pew next to Kurt. He kept his eyes trained straight ahead,

LORI WILDE

his hands clenched in his lap. She wondered what thoughts ran through his mind.

The building smelled like hymnbooks and wax candles. Fabric rustled as ladies scooted across the wooden benches. Several heads pivoted to study her. A large piano crouched to the left of the pulpit.

By the time most of the congregation had filtered in, a man in a black suit went up to the microphone. "Good morning everyone."

"Good morning, Reverend," people chorused.

"We've got a mini-crisis today, folks. Our pianist, Gertie Mae Leery, fell this morning and broke her hip."

The crowd murmured their sympathy.

"Awful. Yes." The preacher shook his balding head. "She's in surgery right now, and she'll be in Room 210 at Rascal General. Please drop by to see her later on or send a card."

Everyone nodded.

"Because of poor Gertie's accident, we're in desperate need of a pianist for today's service. Is anyone willing to be a last-minute substitute?" The microphone squawked. The reverend peered out at the congregation. "Anyone?"

Silence.

"Come on, folks. As a tribute to Gertie Mae. I know some of you are quite talented musicians." He ran a finger around his collar. "This could be your good deed for the week."

Still, no one volunteered.

The preacher sighed. "Well, I suppose we'll have to trudge along a cappella."

"I'll do it." Shocking herself, Bonnie stood and clutched the back of the pew with one hand. Every head in the building turned in her direction.

The reverend looked mildly surprised that someone had taken him up on his plea. "Why, what a nice offer, Miss..."

"Beth," she said firmly, raising her voice high and clear.

She moved down the aisle toward the altar, her pink sundress swishing between her legs.

"Come on up here, Beth. Glad to have you, young lady." Obviously, the preacher didn't recognize her. "We really appreciate this and so does Gertie Mae."

"It's Elizabeth Destiny," someone whispered as Bonnie walked past.

When she reached the altar, the minister shook her hand and led her over to the piano. Holding her head high, she settled herself on the piano bench. Her hands greeted the keys like old friends. To her utter amazement, the instrument came to life under her fingers. Glancing at the hymn book, she began to play "The Old Rugged Cross."

The congregation got to their feet and joined in the song.

Something spiritual swelled inside Bonnie. A powerful experience like nothing she could remember. Her heart thumped in time to the music. Her skin tingled. Quickly she glanced back, saw Hub, Consuelo, Jesse, and Kurt watching her. Kurt looked astonished.

Rapture filled her heart. She smiled and smiled and smiled as her fingers transformed the volatile emotions of the past few days into beautiful, uplifting music.

❧

SOMETHING BIZARRE HAD HAPPENED TO ELIZABETH Destiny.

Kurt simply could not believe his eyes. How was it possible she could suddenly play the piano like an accomplished musician? Could a severe blow to the head really explain such a phenomenon?

And why had she done something so daring as to volunteer to perform before the congregation? If she'd failed, she would have looked like a fool—and Elizabeth Destiny hated to be humiliated.

Stunned, Kurt had no answers.

She looked so lovely, seated on the bench, her body swaying gently, her golden hair twisted in a French plait glimmering in the light slanting through the stained-glass windows.

He listened intently as she coaxed one inspirational tune after another from the aging instrument.

Hub nudged him in the rib cage, telegraphing him a look that clearly said, "What the hell is going on here?"

Kurt shrugged, at a loss for a reasonable explanation.

He was also unable to justify the sudden euphoria boiling inside him. If the accident had altered Elizabeth's brain function to such a radical degree, could this mean a permanent conversion in her personality?

Did he dare hope?

No matter how skeptical he might be, this latest development was much more than Elizabeth's usual attention-seeking tactics. There was no way she could have learned to play the piano with such ease in only six weeks.

Kurt thought about all the ways Elizabeth had changed. Her body was fuller, more rounded, her nose thinner, her lips wider, her hair darker. She smelled of strawberries instead of exotic spice. She was tanned and freckled instead of pale and carefully made-up. Her voice was softer, her words kinder.

And he was incredibly aroused. In a church of all places.

Finally, the reverend took his place in the pulpit, and Elizabeth ended the hymn. She bowed her head, her posture radiating a quiet peacefulness.

Pride rose in Kurt's chest. He adjusted his tie and smiled. Elizabeth's beauty had attracted him in the beginning, and he'd been swept away by her physical charms. Later, when she'd dropped her actress's mask, and her real-self emerged, he'd been appalled at his own gullibility.

Now, something new stirred within him. Calm respect for the woman perched on the stool, and an attraction that plumbed far deeper than surface beauty.

Who was this mysterious woman?

Like polarized magnets, his emotions warred. On the one hand, he wanted Elizabeth as he'd never wanted anyone, yet on the other, she'd hurt him so badly he was terrified to trust her again, despite the apparent changes in her personality.

Clenching his fists, he listened to the sermon without hearing a word, his gaze transfixed on Elizabeth.

He remembered when they'd first met at that party over a year ago. She'd walked up to him, drink in hand, placed an index finger in the middle of his chest, licked her lips, and in a breathless Marilyn Monroe sigh said, "You, Kurt McNally, are my destiny."

Kurt squirmed at the memory.

Hub touched his shoulder. "Easy, Boss. Don't let her lead you down the garden path."

It was uncanny how well Hub knew him. Having spent the last twenty-four years together, sharing most of life's ups and downs, they were as close as two people could be. Hub was right. No matter how much amnesia might have changed Elizabeth Destiny, he could not forget the cruel things she'd done.

A door at the back of the church whispered closed. Kurt barely acknowledged the sound. Someone coughed, heads turned, and murmurs rippled through the crowd.

Hub glanced over his shoulder, then tugged at Kurt's sleeve. "Hold on to your hat, Boss. Look who just walked in."

A forbidding sensation tingled down Kurt's spine. Slowly, he swiveled his head.

There, framed in the morning light, stood his ex-business partner and Elizabeth's former lover, Grant Lewis.

❧❀❧

AFTER THE SERVICE, A CAREFREE GIDDINESS FILLED Bonnie's heart. She hadn't been so happy since she'd awakened from the accident. Coaxing spiritual tunes from the old piano had done wonders for her soul.

She felt rejuvenated, invigorated, energized. And although she didn't actually recall ever having played the piano before, she knew without a doubt that the musical instrument had once played an essential part in her life, despite Kurt's claim that she was tone-deaf.

Walking down the aisle to where Kurt and his friends had been sitting, Bonnie found she couldn't stop grinning. For the first time in three days, her heart floated lighter than a helium-filled hot-air balloon bobbing gaily against its tether.

She passed by a handsome stranger. He smiled at her, but she barely noticed, her gaze searching the crowd for Kurt. The pew they'd been sitting at was vacant.

Where were they?

The stranger rose to his feet behind her.

Frowning, she stopped. In an instant, she was mobbed by people, all chattering at once. Some asked for her autograph; some congratulated her on an exceptional musical performance; others just seemed to want to touch her.

To be polite, Bonnie smiled and nodded, scribbling her signature on prayer books and slips of paper. She fielded numerous questions. Despite the interruptions, she couldn't stop scanning the church for any sign of Kurt.

The minister came over to express his appreciation and introduce her to his family. Patiently, she tried to listen. After about fifteen minutes, the crowd thinned out, and the minister departed. Bonnie looked up to see the handsome man she'd spotted earlier standing to one side, his hands clasped behind his back.

He was about Kurt's height but possessed a leaner build. He had dark hair and darker eyes, but something about his demeanor made her very uncomfortable.

"Hello, Elizabeth," he said, taking her hand in both of his as if he were a campaigning politician. "When did you blow into town?"

Bonnie forced a smile. "I'm sorry, have we met?"

He threw back his head and laughed, revealing capped, bonded teeth. "Oh, that's rich, honey. I know your body intimately, and you'd like to know if we've ever met."

"I had an accident. I'm suffering from traumatic amnesia."

"Oh, so that explains how you got back into McNally's good graces. A stroke of genius, my dear. But then you were always a wily one, and now you're playing the good little church girl to perfection. Got to give credit where credit is due; you're the best, babe."

"If you must address me, I insist you call me Miss Destiny."

"God, I love it! You're great."

The last of the congregation filtered out, leaving Bonnie alone with the stranger. Where was Kurt when she needed him? She gulped and tugged her hand back, but the man held on tighter.

"Please," she said, "let go of me."

"When I heard rumors you'd returned to Rascal, I couldn't believe it. I had to see for myself."

Her chest constricted. Her eyes widened in fear.

"Who are you?" she whispered, trying desperately to wrench her hand from his, but he clung to her like a tick.

"Come on, babe, McNally might be gullible enough to fall for that amnesia schlock but not me."

Bonnie sucked in her breath as realization dawned. This had to be the man she'd had an affair with. Staring at him now, a shudder of revulsion ran through her. How could she ever have found him attractive?

"You're him, aren't you?"

"Grant Lewis in the flesh."

"Please, step away from me," Bonnie said.

"I really like this kinky sex game, darling, very original." He leaned closer, the scent of his musky cologne overwhelming her senses. "You should have let me in on the scheme. I would have been down for it."

"Sir," she said in a thunderous voice. "Unhand me!"

"Keep it up, babe, your acting turns me on. Always has. Remember that time we played 'pirate and damsel in distress'?" Ducking his head, he kissed her with his mouth open.

Angered, Bonnie bit down on his bottom lip. Hard.

"Ouch!" Grant Lewis exclaimed, pulling back and glaring at her. He pressed the back of his hand to his mouth. "What did you do that for?"

"Let's set the record straight, Mr. Lewis," Bonnie said, her chest heaving. "No matter what relationship we might have had in the past, it's over. Completely."

"Oh, I see, playing hard to get."

Bonnie spun on her heels, but he caught her elbow and jerked her into his arms. His dark eyes gleamed.

"Surely you don't want me to scream," she said.

"In church? Give it a go. That might be hot."

"If you don't release me, I'll file sexual harassment charges against you."

"You can't treat me like this, Elizabeth Destiny. I know all your secrets."

"Let me go!" She struggled against him, but he held on.

"Lewis." Kurt's voice was sharp, commanding. "You heard the lady."

They both turned to peer at Kurt who had stepped through a side door. Bonnie's pulse raced. She had never been so happy to see him, despite the angry scowl on his face.

"Turn her loose." Kurt stalked toward them, more imposing than a gunslinger.

Grant Lewis let her go.

Bonnie stumbled away.

The two men squared off, toe-to-toe. Kurt's jaw jutted forward, his body held at attention.

"How far do you want to take this?" Kurt asked, knotting his big hands into fists. Bonnie winced. She hated the thought of these men brawling in church over her.

Lewis raised his palms as if to shield himself from the brunt of Kurt's anger. "Hey, man, obviously I made a mistake."

"Obviously."

"I didn't know she had amnesia."

"Well, now you do." Kurt moved forward like a panther ready to pounce.

"I'll be going." Lewis took a step backward.

"You do that."

Lewis turned and fled.

Stony-faced, Kurt met Bonnie's eyes. "Let's go."

Bonnie splayed a palm across her chest. "You don't think I encouraged him, do you?"

"This isn't the time nor place for this discussion." He turned on his heels.

"Wait." Bonnie scurried after him. "We need to talk about what just happened."

"Drop it, okay?"

Her heart sank to her stomach; her earlier euphoria evaporated. When it seemed as if she were making progress in her bid to rekindle her relationship with Kurt, Grant Lewis had happened along to send them right back to square one.

How could she convince Kurt she was not interested in the man? How could she make him believe that he was the only one she cared about? How could she ever hope to regain his trust?

Sadness enveloped her at the monumental task. She followed him into the bright July sunlight, vowing to herself she would not give up trying because without hope, nothing was possible.

❧ 10 ❧

Kurt knew Elizabeth had not encouraged Grant Lewis. *That* was the only reason he'd rescued her.

Before the services had ended, he'd sent the others outside, then secreted himself in one of the empty Bible study rooms. Leaving the door slightly ajar, he'd watched her bounce exuberantly down the aisle, ignoring Lewis completely.

Her behavior had given credence to her amnesia claim. And whether it was logical or not, he had believed her.

In fact, she hadn't even acknowledged Lewis until he'd approached her. Kurt had intently studied her face, saw no flicker of recognition when Lewis had greeted her, and she'd seemed genuinely alarmed when the man kissed her.

Kurt gritted his teeth. The old jealousy wound around his gut like a venomous snake. Her betrayal had cut him to the quick, but how could he hold it against her now when she didn't even remember the episode?

In his mind, he saw it all again. Elizabeth, his fiancée, and Grant, his business partner, locked in the throes of love-making right in the middle of his bed. And the awful thing

97

was when he'd confronted them, Elizabeth had laughed in his face. How could he have been so blind to the true nature of both his business partner and his fiancée?

A heated flush ran up his neck.

"Kurt?"

He stopped outside the church, his gaze scanning the grounds for Hub. From behind him, Beth touched his shoulder.

Kurt turned to face her. Right now, he wanted to be anywhere but here, dealing with this.

"I'm so sorry," she whispered.

"You did nothing wrong."

"This time. I'm apologizing for the past. I can't believe I, er, did anything with that person."

"I'm sorry he bothered you."

"How could I have been with a man like that?"

"Better question, how could I have been in business with him?"

"Don't blame yourself. We were at fault. Not you."

He nodded, not knowing what else to say. A gentle breeze blew, lifting her pink sundress around her legs. God, she was more beautiful than ever. The sun beat down. Perspiration gathered along his collar.

"Help me, Kurt," she whispered.

"How?"

"Help me get my memory back."

"Are you sure that's what you want?"

Beth nodded. "You don't know how completely frustrating it is not to remember anything. I feel so vulnerable."

"You might not like what you discover," he said.

"I don't imagine I will, but I've got to know. I have to find out why I can play the piano, why I have memories of an aunt you say doesn't exist. Will you help me?"

He hesitated.

"It'll be painful for us both, but I can't do it alone." She reached out and took his hand, giving it a squeeze. "Please."

"Yeah, okay." Lord, he could refuse her nothing. "Tomorrow we'll go see Dr. Freely again."

"Promise?" Her blue eyes pleaded with him for understanding.

"I promise," Kurt uttered the words, wondering what in the world he'd committed himself to uncover.

☙❧

BONNIE GRASPED KURT'S HAND AS THEY ENTERED DR. Freely's office on Monday morning. His reassuring squeeze buoyed her mood.

The doctor's waiting area was a large, airy room splashed with sunlight from floor-to-ceiling windows. Abstract murals adorned the walls. The furniture was plush and new. Pots of Benjamin Ficus, rubber trees, and corn plants lent an outdoorsy atmosphere.

After they checked in at the receptionist desk, Kurt took Bonnie's elbow and guided her over to a leather sofa in the corner near a magazine rack. She settled into the soft seat and sighed.

"Are you okay?" Kurt asked, concern in his voice.

"Fine."

Bonnie offered him a dazzling smile. Ever since that episode with Grant Lewis the day before, Kurt had been very solicitous. She desperately wanted to court his kindness.

"Would you like a magazine?" he asked.

"Yes."

Kurt stretched to reach the magazine rack, his long legs flexing as he half rose from his seat. Bonnie couldn't stop herself from staring at the sight of his faded blue jeans molding tightly against his firm backside.

Heavens!

He plopped *People* in her lap.

"Er...could I have *Better Homes and Gardens* please?"

One eyebrow shot up on his forehead. "Your tastes have changed."

Leaning over once more, he exchanged magazines. Bonnie used the opportunity to examine his rear end again. A silly smile curled her lips.

"Here you go."

"Thanks."

He nestled back against the sofa, opened a copy of *Forbes*, and rested the ankle of his left leg against his right knee. Bonnie flipped through her magazine, but it didn't hold her interest. She kept sneaking glances at Kurt, admiring the way the sun glinted off the golden highlights in his light-brown hair.

"What?" he asked.

"Nothing." Bonnie dropped her gaze.

"Something on my face?"

Besides that beautiful mouth, those piercing eyes, that proud nose? She shook her head.

"You want another magazine?"

"No, thanks."

She had to stop staring at him like a lovesick schoolgirl. But what she wouldn't give to run her fingers through his silky hair, to play his thoroughly male body like piano keys, to run her tongue along those full lips.

Bonnie squinted, searching the room for something to distract her from such dangerous thoughts. She studied an elderly woman sitting across from them and a well-dressed young man seated by the window.

"Your vision has been impaired since the accident, hasn't it?" Kurt observed. "You can't see at a distance."

"Yes."

"We'll get Dr. Freely to examine your eyes. I bet you need glasses."

"Glasses?"

"Of course, I suppose you'll want contact lenses."

Bonnie shrugged. "Glasses will be all right."

"Until you go back to making movies."

His remark startled her. Actually, the thought of making movies hadn't entered her mind. She'd been too busy trying to put her life back together to even consider her career. Her career. It sounded so strange.

Bonnie took a deep breath. "I don't know if I want to go back to acting."

"What? You? Give up acting? Might as well ask a bird not to fly."

"The thought leaves me cold. Apparently, I've always put my career ahead of everything else."

"That's the way it has to be in your field."

"People, relationships are more important than any career. You're important to me, Kurt." Although she'd been thinking these things, she hadn't intended on saying them.

"Acting means everything to you, Elizabeth. I accepted that about you from the beginning of our relationship. When you get your memory back, you'll be on the next plane to Los Angeles."

"I don't think so."

"Wait and see."

"What if I don't get my memory back?"

"What do you mean?"

"Can I stay in Rascal, with you?" Bonnie's heart raced as she waited for his answer. Would he allow her to remain with him?

"Your memory will return," he replied gruffly.

"What if it doesn't?" she repeated.

"Elizabeth Destiny," the office nurse called out, saving Kurt from answering her question.

They rose together, leaving their magazines on the coffee table, and followed the nurse down a corridor.

"In here," the nurse said, leading them into an exam room. "Dr. Freely will be with you momentarily."

Bonnie climbed onto the examination table while Kurt seated himself on a three-legged rolling stool. Stainless-steel instruments were lined up on a nearby cabinet. A medical chart depicting the nerves of the human body hung on the wall. Two black stethoscopes dangled from a hook on the back of the door.

She swung her legs against the examination table, anxiously wanting to resume their conversation, but Kurt's body language warned her off. He sat with his knees together, his feet planted on the floor, his arms folded tightly across his chest.

A quick rap at the door and Dr. Freely came into the room. "Hello, Ms. Destiny." She beamed.

Bonnie smiled back, encouraged.

"Mr. McNally." The doctor nodded at Kurt.

"Doctor Freely," Kurt said.

"My nurse tells me you've been having some rather bizarre symptoms," Dr. Freely said, placing both hands on Bonnie's shoulders.

"Bizarre is an understatement," Kurt mumbled.

"Tell me about them." The physician removed her bandage and tenderly inspected Bonnie's head wound.

"I can play the piano," Bonnie replied.

The doctor arched an eyebrow. "Yes?"

"Before the accident, she was tone-deaf." Kurt got to his feet and leaned one shoulder against the wall.

"Ah."

"Is that common?"

"Well, no," Dr. Freely admitted, "but it's not out of the question."

"How could it be that I've never played a musical instrument before and now I'm proficient?" Bonnie asked.

"The brain is a complex and mysterious organ."

"In other words, you don't have a clue," Kurt said.

"Perhaps she played a musical instrument as a child, is that possible?" Dr. Freely asked.

Bonnie shrugged. "Who knows. I don't remember."

"There are other things, too," Kurt said, "like her vision. Elizabeth used to have the eyesight of an eagle; now she can barely see across your waiting room."

"Hmm." The doctor tapped her chin with an index finger. "You were struck on the temple. That could explain the vision problems. I think you should see an ophthalmologist."

"Is my vision permanently damaged?"

"Possibly," Dr. Freely mused. "I'm sorry."

Bonnie's bottom lip trembled. Until this moment, she hadn't realized how nervous she was.

"Have you had any memory flashes?" Dr. Freely pulled a reflex hammer from her pocket and tested Bonnie's reflexes.

Pursing her lips, Bonnie blew out her breath. "Sort of. It's weird."

"Tell me."

She looked to Kurt, and he nodded his head. Bolstered, she told Dr. Freely about the strange memory she'd had at the drugstore in Rascal. "The curious thing is, Kurt tells me I have no aunts. How can I remember someone who never existed?"

"Could you have recalled a scene from some movie you acted in? Since you're an actress, movie memories could be as real to you as any others."

The theory enticed her. She hadn't thought of that explanation. Raising her eyes, she met Kurt's steady gaze. "Did I ever appear in a movie with a scene in a drugstore?"

"Yeah." Kurt nodded. "*Some Can Love.*"

"I don't remember it."

"We can stream it on Netflix."

"That's a marvelous idea," Dr. Freely said. "Show Elizabeth her movies. They could be a great tool in helping her regain her memory."

"Is there anything else we can do to jog my memory?" Bonnie leaned forward, suddenly very excited. No matter how painful knowing the truth about herself might be, it was a thousand times better than living in this strange limbo land.

"Yes." Dr. Freely shifted her attention to Kurt. "Take her places you've been before. Ask her specific questions. Introduce her to people she once knew."

"We've been doing that," Kurt said.

"Keep trying. It'll take a while."

"And if that doesn't work?"

"As a last resort, you could try hypnosis, but that's a stretch," Dr. Freely said.

"What if my memory doesn't return?" Bonnie asked timidly, finding the possibility terrifying on the one hand, yet strangely liberating on the other. If her memory loss was permanent, she and Kurt could start their relationship fresh, as if the past had never existed.

"Give it a month. If you haven't started to remember anything, we'll do more tests."

"A month!" Kurt exclaimed.

Wounded, Bonnie looked away. Apparently, he did not want her hanging around that long, but could she really blame him?

"Why not do the tests now?" Kurt asked.

Dr. Freely frowned. "It takes time to heal from amnesia. I'd prefer to wait on other testing. No point in putting her through the trouble and expense of more testing this early in the game."

"How do you feel about that, Elizabeth?" Kurt moved toward her.

She nodded. "I'm good with waiting."

"What are the chances her memory loss is permanent?" Kurt asked.

"That's difficult to determine."

"Can you give us percentages?" he asked.

Us. A sudden thrill rushed through her. As if Kurt consider her amnesia his problem as well.

"Well..." Dr. Freely said, "I'd estimate ninety percent of patients regain most of their memories eventually."

"Eventually?"

"I've had one patient whose amnesia lasted twenty years."

"Twenty years," Bonnie whispered at the terrifying thought and wadded her hands into tight fists. Twenty years!

"How did that person finally regain his or her memory?" Kurt stepped over and rested a reassuring hand on her shoulder.

For the first time since she'd awakened on that hard cement sidewalk, dazed and in pain, she felt as if she weren't completely alone.

"A spontaneous occurrence."

"Is that how most memories return?" Bonnie asked.

The doctor nodded. "Just give it time, Ms. Destiny."

Time. Something she didn't possess a lot of. Kurt had made it perfectly clear her stay at the ranch was limited. How long before he asked her to leave? The idea of being left to fend for herself had fear's icy fingers squeezing her heart.

"Any other questions?" Dr. Freely rested her hand on the doorknob.

Bonnie shook her head, too worried to think clearly.

"If you have any problems, call my office, day or night.

The answering service will contact me if it's after business hours. In the meantime, continue exploring your past with Mr. McNally."

Exploring the past with Kurt. The prospect should have been exciting. Instead, Bonnie was frightened of what she might discover.

"My nurse will give you a referral to an ophthalmologist. She'll make sure to get you an appointment this afternoon," the physician said.

"Thank you," Bonnie mumbled.

"It's going to be all right, Elizabeth," Kurt said after Dr. Freely had left the room. "You'll see. Before you know it, you'll be back making movies without giving me a second thought."

"That's not what I want."

"Sure it is."

Bonnie shook her head violently. "I want to stay in Rascal with you."

He took her hand and helped her down from the examination table. "That's only because you're confused right now. Once your memory comes back, things will look very different."

"I don't want my memory back," she said vehemently.

"Yes, you do."

"Not if it means I have to lose you."

Their eyes met, caught.

Bonnie exhaled. Something stirred deep within her, something she'd never experienced before. Or at least nothing she could remember experiencing.

"You don't really want me," he said gruffly. "You're just feeling vulnerable right now."

"Yes, I do."

His hand tightened around hers. She saw pain flicker in his eyes and knew she was the cause.

"Let's take each day one step at a time, Elizabeth."

"Things are going to be different between us, Kurt, I swear it."

"No," he said, roughly tugging his hands from hers. "Don't make promises you can't keep." And with that, he pivoted on his heels and stalked from the examining room, leaving Bonnie more confused than ever.

❧ 11 ❧

While they waited on Elizabeth's ophthalmology appointment, Kurt took her to lunch at the Bluebird Cafe on The River Walk. They sat outside beneath an orange-and-green umbrella and watched the tourists walked by.

A warm breeze gusted. Brightly colored pansies danced in wooden planter boxes. Blue jays cawed from pecan trees. A bluebird windsock flapped around a metal pole mounted overhead. At the tables around them, men and women wearing suits and carrying briefcases discussed business. Silverware clattered, and muted music wafted over the sound system.

It should have been a pleasant interlude. Instead, a stony silence stretched between them. Kurt didn't know what to say. He hadn't meant to hurt her feelings back there in Dr. Freely's office. Truth be told, he longed to have this sweet, vulnerable, piano-playing "Beth" stay with him forever.

And that's what scared him.

Although he was convinced she wasn't acting, he still could not risk losing his heart to her again. The first time around, Elizabeth tricked him, and he'd found out the hard way what a cold, calculating woman hid behind her public facade.

This time, she was different. But when her memory returned, he'd be back where he started. No. He just would not let himself care about her, no matter how beguiling she appeared.

They had ordered club sandwiches and iced tea, but Elizabeth just picked at her food, tearing the crust from the whole wheat bread and lining it along the edges of her plate. Kurt's appetite had vanished as well. He emptied two sugar packets into his tea glass and stirred.

"We'll watch some of your movies tonight," he said.

"Okay." She stared down at her plate, her shoulders moving slightly.

"Beth?"

"Wh-what," she whispered.

"Are you crying?"

"N-no."

"Look at me."

She shook her head.

He reached across the table and lifted her chin. Tears webbed her eyelashes, and the sight slugged him in the gut. Oh, jeez, why did Beth have to be so lovable?

"Talk to me."

"I've lost so much." She sighed. "And put you through immeasurable pain. There's no way I can ever make up for that."

"I survived," Kurt said gruffly, appalled by the sudden urge to pull her into his arms and kiss her until the waiter had to pry them apart.

He couldn't stop thinking how lovely it would feel to hug her tender flesh to his chest, to run his fingers through her silky blond hair, to make love to her slow, soft, and natural.

Instead, he sipped his tea and tried to chase the enticing image from his mind.

Pity, he told himself. He felt sorry for her, but that was it.

Elizabeth swiped her eyes with the back of her hands. Uncharacteristically, her fingernails were short and bare. Before the accident, she'd worn long, red, sculpted nails. Funny, he'd never noticed what tiny fingers she had. And those wrists! Exposed, pale and dainty. He knew if he were to press his nose against those sweet wrists, the aroma of wild strawberries would mangle his senses.

Stop it, McNally. Don't you dare go there.

Clearing his throat, he peeked at his watch, desperate for any distraction to wrench his gaze from Elizabeth's lovely face.

"Your eye appointment's in thirty minutes; you ready to go?"

"Yes."

He signaled the waiter for their check and pushed back his chair.

"I'm keeping a tab of exactly how much I owe you. I promise to pay you back as soon as something is resolved." She touched her temple to indicate her amnesia.

"I've plenty of money, Elizabeth."

"That's not the point. I don't want to owe you anything."

"Don't worry, you don't owe me anything," he said brusquely.

Strangely enough, her comment hurt. Elizabeth's strong independence had always bothered him. Because of his childhood—being abandoned by his mother at age ten, never knowing his father, growing up in an orphanage—he had always possessed a poignant longing to be part of a close couple. To have a family of his own.

A puzzled expression crossed her face, but Elizabeth said nothing, she just followed him out of the restaurant. Kurt drove to the ophthalmologist office and waited in the lobby while she had her eyes examined.

He rang his office on his cell phone, spent several minutes working out the details of an investment proposal, then called to check on the progress of a Habitat For Humanity project. But business could not keep his mind off Beth. He pocketed the phone and got to his feet, his mind restless and unsettled.

He paced and fretted. His emotions clashed and conflicted. On the one hand, he knew it was absolutely idiotic to think there could possibly be a future with Elizabeth, yet whenever she smiled at him, his heart melted, and he found himself hoping against hope that somehow, someway this change in her could be permanent.

"You're a damned fool, McNally," he growled under his breath.

A startled lady slanted him a suspicious look, picked up her purse, and moved across the room.

By the time Elizabeth emerged from the doctor's office, Kurt had made a decision. No matter how appealing she might be, no matter how she might tug at his heartstrings, he would not allow himself to romanticize her amnesia.

"Well?" Kurt raised his eyebrows when she joined him in the waiting room.

"I'm nearsighted. Myopic."

"Caused by the accident?"

"That's the funny thing," Bonnie said. "He said the accident most likely didn't cause it. He said I've probably needed glasses for years."

"Weird. You used to be able to spot things at a distance before anyone else. Nearsighted people can't do that."

Bonnie shrugged. "He didn't say it was impossible for the accident to have caused my vision problem. Just unlikely." She waved a prescription. "I've got to get glasses. Will you help me pick out a pair?"

"Wouldn't you rather have contact lenses?"

Bonnie made a face. "I don't know if I can stick things in my eyes."

"All right then, let's do this."

***

KURT SHOVED HIS HANDS INTO THE POCKETS OF HIS JEANS. He seemed uncomfortable. He was the hardest man to figure out. One minute she felt as if he were starting to open up to her, letting down his guard a fraction. While they were in Dr. Freely's office, he'd been kind and solicitous. But by lunch, he'd withdrawn from her again. She watched him distance himself, shifting his body away from her and averting his eyes.

One step forward, two steps back. Would they ever reach the point where they could communicate honestly and openly? Bonnie was beginning to doubt it. If only he trusted her.

If only...

She shook her head. Regrets were useless. Much more sensible to accept things as they were and move on, but oh! How part of her wanted to mend the past.

What would happen, she wondered, if she tried to seduce him?

The idea sent a thrill shooting through her veins. Did she dare? Gulping, she gave him a sidelong glance.

They walked next door to the optical center. Bonnie noticed Kurt kept a safe distance between them. It would be darned hard seducing him if he insisted on remaining so aloof. Sadness plummeted in her stomach like an elevator settling to the basement floor.

She had to stop wishing for the impossible. When would she get it through her thick skull that Kurt simply was not interested in reestablishing their relationship?

The store smelled of fresh paint and new carpet. A saleswoman greeted them with a cheery smile and ushered them around the store before leaving them to make their purchase in peace.

"They've got a big selection," Kurt said. Crowded display cases lined the walls, exhibiting every type of frame available.

"Too many choices," Bonnie muttered.

Kurt looked at her. "You need frames in a soft color. Something that won't overwhelm your delicate features."

A heated flush spread up Bonnie's neck at his compliment. Kurt picked up a pair of pale gray frames.

"Here," he said, "try these."

She raised her face. He slid the glasses over her ears, his large fingers grazing her cheeks. His touch sent a throbbing warmth tingling over her skin, and Bonnie sucked in her breath.

He took a step back and tilted his head. "Nope. Too light."

Hastily, before he could touch her again, Bonnie removed the frames and handed them to him. She dropped her gaze so he couldn't read the confusion in her eyes. How she wanted to release the tether from her heart and allow herself to love him, but she didn't dare.

"How about these?" He reached for a light-brown pair.

Snatching the frames from his hand, she slipped them on.

"Too square."

"What do you think about wire frames?" Bonnie returned the brown pair to the display case and retrieved another pair of glasses.

"I like them. Very intellectual-looking."

She turned to peer at herself in the mirror and smiled. She did look somewhat scholarly.

Kurt reached over and brushed her bangs from her forehead. He stood only inches away, his body radiating dangerous heat. Did the man have any idea what he did to her? Bonnie's knees wobbled like a jar of peach preserves.

"Get them," he said, his voice resonating low and deep. "They're perfect."

"I could pass for a schoolteacher instead of an actress," she said, twisting her hair into a bun and holding it in place on top of her head.

"A very sexy schoolteacher," he muttered, his breath warm against the back of her neck. Bonnie bit down on her bottom lip to keep from shivering.

"A good way to hide from autograph-seeking fans," she mused.

"Since when did you ever shy from attention?" Kurt teased.

"Since the accident."

"I hate to say it, Beth, but getting hit on the head seems to be the best thing that ever happened to you."

"Oh, yeah?" She grinned, heartened by his teasing tone.

"Yeah," he whispered. "I can't believe you're really you." He leaned forward and peered at her from half-lidded eyes, overt sexuality oozing from every pore in his body.

Would she ever understand this man? One minute he was grouchy and sullen, the next affectionate and teasing. Had he always been so mercurial or was it his reaction to her?

He turned his head. The fluorescent lighting illuminated his strong jaw and proud, regal nose, and his hair glowed a golden bronze.

His reaction to her might be mutable, changing in an instant, but her response to him had been the same from the moment he'd walked into her hospital room. She'd wanted him. Plain and simple. Wanted to salvage their relationship no matter what the cost.

"You're more beautiful than ever."

His words lent wings to her soul. *Maybe. Maybe. Maybe.*

She had a sudden, intense desire to kiss him. Hard. Wet. Long.

Bonnie gulped and lowered her arms, allowing her hair to swing loose around her shoulders. In the mirror, she saw Kurt observing her. A strange gleam lit his hazel eyes. A gleam that hinted at a lurking passion.

Oh my! Shocked, she realized he was thinking the same thing she was thinking.

Panic flooded her. Much as she wanted him to kiss her again, could she handle anything more profound? Amnesia had robbed her of so many memories. Unfortunately, the whack on the side of the head had stolen all recall of their lovemaking. Terrified, Bonnie realized she had no idea how to pleasure a man.

Good heavens, here she'd been plotting to seduce him and win him back, and now that he seemed receptive, she didn't know how to take things to the next level. Hands trembling, she curled her fingers around the wire-rimmed glasses.

Ducking her head, she pivoted and almost ran to the front counter. One thing was suddenly obvious. If she hoped to get Kurt McNally in bed, she'd have to learn what to do once she got him there.

❧ 12 ❧

Beth looked cute with those glasses perched on her tiny nose, Kurt thought as he ushered her up the sidewalk and into his house. Damn cute.

Her cheeks were flushed; her blue eyes sparkled; her blond hair curled provocatively below her shoulders. The denim romper she wore fit her to perfection, nipping in at her slender waist, flaring over her rounded hips, accentuating her tanned legs. Kurt couldn't help admiring the view.

You're getting in deep, McNally. Watch your step. The life you save may be your own.

But no amount of coaching could change the feeling growing in his chest. A sensation that rattled him more than he cared to admit, an odd emotion, unlike anything he'd ever experienced. When he tried to compare it to the feelings he'd had at the beginning of his courtship with Elizabeth, he was at a loss.

The first time he'd seen Elizabeth, he'd been immediately aroused by her beauty, her poise, her cool sophistication. The physical attraction had been hard and swift. At the time, he'd mistaken those feelings for love when in reality it had been plain old-fashioned lust. What he felt for her now was completely different.

He still wanted her. Oh, yes! Perhaps more so. Just thinking of those sweet lips, her strawberries and cream scent, her soft, pliant flesh, sent a heated rush hurtling throughout his lower anatomy.

No, what troubled him were the other sensations—this urge to protect her, his desire to wrap her in his arms when she cried and kiss away her tears, the strong need to help her regain her memory despite the unsettling revelations it was sure to bring.

"Would you like to watch one of your movies?" he asked, flicking on the light in the TV room.

"I don't want to keep you from your work," she said.

Lord, how she'd changed. Kurt remembered a petulant, pouting Elizabeth who complained whenever he immersed himself in his job. Now, here she was encouraging him.

"It'll keep," he said gruffly. "Getting your memory back is more important right now. Which one shall we watch?"

"The one you spoke of before. The one with the drugstore soda fountain in it."

"*Some Can Love*. You won an Oscar for your role as Mary Duncan, a girl from the wrong side of the tracks. Remember?"

Beth shook her head. "No."

Kurt turned on the TV.

"How many movies have I made?" Beth asked, wandering aimlessly around the room.

"Sixteen."

"That many?"

"You've been acting since you were nineteen," he replied, connecting to Netflix.

She sighed. "I wish I could remember."

"That's what we're working on. Here, take this." Kurt

thrust the remote control in her hand, his gaze lingering on the forlorn expression skewing her face. "Have a seat. I'll go microwave some popcorn and be back in a second."

He dimmed the lights as he went out of the room, leaving Elizabeth to settle onto the couch. His heart strummed a little faster, but he didn't know why.

Consuelo was cleaning out the refrigerator. "Where's Elizabeth?" she asked.

"Watching *Some Can Love*. The doctor recommended it. I'm nuking us some popcorn." Kurt took the popcorn from the pantry.

"Us?" Consuelo peered at him.

"Yeah. I thought I'd help her."

"Kurt..."

"I know, I know." He raised his palms in a defensive gesture. "Don't light into me, Consuelo."

"Be careful," she warned.

"Beth really is different," Kurt said, leaning against the kitchen counter.

"Please, Kurt, you can't be one hundred percent sure she's not acting."

"You didn't see her with Grant Lewis at church. She seemed totally frightened of him. I know she didn't recognize him."

"I don't want her to hurt you again."

The aroma of hot popcorn filled the room. Kurt shifted his weight. Consuelo was merely voicing his own concerns.

"She does seem much sweeter," Consuelo conceded. "Very different. If I didn't know better, I'd swear she was another person."

Kurt nodded, a tightness squeezing his stomach. Yes, Beth was sweeter and kinder and more honest.

"But what happens when she gets her memory back?"

Consuelo tossed half a head of shriveled iceberg lettuce into the garbage pail.

"Then she'll go back to Los Angeles." Kurt shrugged.

"You can't fool me."

"What do you mean?"

"You're falling for her again."

Kurt snorted. "I am not."

"I see it in your eyes."

"Don't be ridiculous, Consuelo." But his heart lurched. He was most definitely not falling for Elizabeth Destiny. He just felt sorry for her. Helping her was no different than helping the homeless acquire shelter or assisting the sick to find medical treatment.

"Be careful," she warned again. "You know how you get when you have a cause to champion."

BONNIE'S EYES WERE GLUED TO THE TV SCREEN. FROM THE moment the credits started to roll, she'd been hooked. Something about this felt so familiar, yet she couldn't pinpoint what it was. She didn't really remember making the movie or even viewing it. No. It was something else. The act of snuggling into the sofa, watching the story unfold, stirred inside her a cozy feeling of comfort and security.

The fragrant smell of crisp popcorn preceded Kurt into the room. Bonnie hit the "pause" button and smiled.

He carried two glasses of cola and a bowl of popcorn on a tray. She scooted over and patted the cushion beside her. Kurt set the drinks on the coffee table and eased down next to her, putting the popcorn bowl between them.

"Ready?"

"Uh-huh."

She hit the "pause" button again, and the soundtrack came to life.

"When did this movie come out?" she whispered, reaching for a handful of buttery popcorn. Her elbow accidentally grazed his thigh, and she sucked in her breath at the rough feel of denim.

"Three years ago."

On-screen the camera panned a cracked sidewalk in a squalid neighborhood. The soundtrack played "Rock Around The Clock." The cars and clothing indicated the film was set in the late fifties.

"Here you come." Kurt pointed at the screen. He leaned forward, his face animated. "I've got to hand it to you, Beth, nobody makes an entrance like you do."

He's excited, Bonnie thought, and her heart skipped a beat. Excited by *her* on-screen image. Why couldn't he respond to her in the flesh with the same enthusiasm?

Kurt munched a mouthful of popcorn, and Bonnie followed his stare. She saw herself saunter down the sidewalk, her hips swaying, her breasts straining against her tight sweater.

Bonnie glanced down at her own chest. She wasn't that well-endowed. Frowning, she attributed the difference to the magic of Hollywood.

Overgrown boys in leather jackets and ducktails whistled at her as she rounded the corner. She puckered her lips and blew them a kiss as steamy as any Marilyn Monroe would have dished up.

Embarrassed, Bonnie hid her face with a couch pillow. So odd to see herself on the screen like this and not remember a minute of it. Not just odd, but weird. The woman in the movie was a complete stranger.

"Beth?" Kurt set the popcorn on the table and turned his body toward her. "What's wrong?"

She lowered the pillow and met his stare. "She's not me."

"What do you mean?"

"I don't move like that."

"Sweetheart, you were acting."

Sweetheart? Where had that come from? The word sent a thrill pulsing through her veins.

"It's more than that."

"I don't understand."

"Nothing feels right. Maybe we should turn it off."

"I can't begin to imagine what you must be going through," he sympathized. "But let's keep watching; maybe something will trigger your recall."

Bonnie nodded and forced herself to concentrate on the movie. But Kurt's presence was too distracting. Every time she tried to follow the storyline, she found her gaze drifting to study the contours of his rugged face, her nose twitching to breathe in his scent.

Kurt rested his arm on the back of the sofa. If she leaned back against it, her nape would touch his firm muscles.

"Here," he said, moving his arm forward until it gently touched her shoulder. Bonnie thought she'd sink through the floor with sheer joy. "Here comes the part where you enter the drugstore. See if any of this matches your memory."

Try as she might, she could not focus on the screen. She pushed her glasses up on her nose and tried to pay attention, but all she could think about was the sound of Kurt's steady breathing, the smell of his spicy cologne mixing with the aroma of popcorn, the exhilarating feel of his hand against her skin.

He began to rub his thumb steadily across her back, his fingers kneading her shoulders. Bonnie gulped, fused to the spot by his intoxicating caress. What had gotten into him? Was he physically aroused by her image on the screen?

"Well?" he asked huskily.

Her eyes drifted half closed. "Huh?"

"Did that scene match the memory you experienced in the drugstore on Saturday?"

"No. I remembered being a little girl with my Aunt June working the soda fountain." Bonnie shook her head at the TV. "Nothing like what's in the movie."

"That's interesting." Kurt continued massaging her shoulder.

The story on-screen played out, but Bonnie's attention lay elsewhere. She didn't care about the actress who looked so much like herself yet felt like a completely different person. She didn't care about the handsome young movie hero grinning at her on-camera persona. At this moment, she didn't even care about her amnesia. Only one thing dominated her mind—Kurt McNally and his magic hands.

"Do you remember Lance Westwood?" he asked.

"Who?" Bonnie almost purred from the delicious sensations.

"Your costar."

"Should I?"

"You two had a love affair."

"We did?" Bonnie frowned.

"In fact, you'd just broken up with him when we met."

Bonnie studied the young actor on the screen. Lance Westwood was much too handsome. Perfect hair, perfect teeth, perfect muscles. She vastly preferred Kurt. He looked like a real man, not some soft, pretty boy.

"Nope," Bonnie said. "Don't remember him."

"I never could figure out why you went out with me after dating a guy like that."

"You felt insecure? Heavens, Kurt, you're twice the man he is."

Kurt's face flushed. "Later on, of course, I found out why you wanted me."

"What do you mean?"

"I know you don't remember any of this, Beth, but you should know the truth. You were marrying me for publicity and money."

Bonnie rounded her shoulders and lowered her head. "Was I really so mercenary?"

"I'm afraid so."

"You don't know how sorry I am."

"I believe you." Kurt pulled her into the curve of his arm. "I just wish it hadn't taken an accident to bring out your good side."

"Me, either."

"Maybe when you get your memory back, you'll have learned something from this experience. Maybe this all happened for a reason."

"I'd like to believe that," she said, her heart thumping faster as she gazed into his hazel eyes.

"Me too," he whispered softly, his mouth very close to her cheek.

What was he saying? Had her efforts to prove herself a changed woman actually paid off? Could he possibly be considering a renewal of their relationship? The biggest question, was she ready for this?

Unnerved, Bonnie leaned forward and reached for her cola.

Lifting the glass to her lips, she stared straight ahead, pretending to be engrossed with the action on the screen. Lance Westwood was toying languidly with a lock of Elizabeth Destiny's hair, his gaze fixed on her ample chest.

"This is where he kisses you," Kurt whispered.

Heated embarrassment splashed through her like ice water, startling and unexpected. Bonnie squirmed as Lance's lips came down hard on Elizabeth's mouth.

Beside her, she heard Kurt inhale raggedly.

"I get jealous watching another man kiss you," he confessed. "Especially when that man used to be your lover."

"Take heart," she said, trying her best to lighten the moment. "I don't remember anyone's kisses but yours."

"Hey," Kurt said, leaning nearer. "If it means all other men have been blocked from your mind, I think I like this amnesia stuff."

His arm still rested across her shoulder. Bonnie clutched her cola glass between her fingers.

Kiss me, she thought. *Kiss me now. Kiss me hard. Kiss me long.* Bonnie caught her breath, waiting.

Kurt hesitated. She saw desire written on his face warring with self-control.

Her teeth parted. His Adam's apple bobbed.

She ran her tongue along her lips.

Reaching up, he removed her glasses, folded them and set them on the coffee table, then he slipped the drink from her hand and settled it beside her glasses. Leaning back, he tightened his grip.

"Beth," he whispered and buried his nose in her hair.

Bonnie closed her eyes and cherished the sound of his voice. He lightly pressed his lips to her ear, and a corresponding shiver raced down her spine.

He painted a trail of moist kisses down her jaw.

Bonnie groaned and tilted her head.

He ended at her chin, his beard stubble raking against her skin.

"Kurt," Bonnie breathed, feeling as if she'd just been given the keys to heaven.

"Excuse me."

They leaped apart, both of them swiveling their heads to stare at Consuelo standing in the doorway, arms akimbo.

Bonnie raised a hand to her lips. Kurt looked chagrined.

"I hate to interrupt your...movie." Consuelo raised one

eyebrow. "But Hub's got a problem he needs to discuss with you, Kurt."

"Sure, sure." Kurt sprung up from the couch. He busied himself brushing wrinkles from his chambray shirt, carefully avoiding Bonnie's eyes. "Be right there."

Briefly, he turned back to Bonnie. "Keep watching," he said, "I'm sure you'll remember something."

Then he disappeared out the door, looking very relieved to make his escape.

13

Kurt couldn't say why he'd started rubbing Elizabeth's shoulders, but once he started, he'd been unable to stop, drawn inexplicably to her natural warmth. Weird. He'd always considered Elizabeth a supremely cool person, but that last kiss had changed his mind. His lips felt as if they'd been seared by a blowtorch.

Good thing Consuelo had interrupted when she had. Her appearance had snapped him back to earth. Damn, why did Beth have to be so physically desirable? Her intoxicating scent, those innocent blue eyes, that petite little nose spelled nothing but trouble.

The woman confused him to no end. When Dr. Freely had first called about Elizabeth and her accident, Kurt had been adamantly opposed to bringing her to the ranch. If anyone had told him four days later he'd be wanting her to stay, he would have snorted derisively.

But that's actually what he did want.

Be real, McNally. No matter how nice, how sweet, how perfect she seems now, all that will change the minute her memory returns.

So why on earth was he trying to help her remember? If he

were smart, he'd avoid her as much as possible. He was opening himself up for a heap of heartache every time he gazed at her, touched her, kissed her. No matter how much he resolved to stay away, he found himself tempted.

Kurt stalked across the yard to where Hub stood silhouetted in the barn doorway. "What's up?"

"Just got a call," Hub said, "we're two peach pickers short for tomorrow's harvest."

Groaning, Kurt ran a hand through his hair. "What happened?"

"One of the harvesters fell off the back of a truck over at the Double W and broke his leg."

"And?"

"Jesse's mother's sick. He's gotta go home."

Kurt swore and kneaded his brow. "I'm sorry to hear that."

"Where are we gonna find the extra hands at this late date?"

"I don't know."

Hub toyed with a pitchfork. "Almost everyone I can think of is already spoken for."

"What about that guy we hired last year?" Kurt snapped his fingers. "What was his name?"

"I know who you mean. He left the state."

"Damn."

"Looks like you're going to have to swallow your pride and take Elizabeth up on her offer."

"What offer is that?"

"Remember, she said she wanted to help with the harvest."

Kurt snorted. "Not very likely."

"Why not? She's surely different, Boss. I will concede that point. If she really wants to help, I say put her to work. Put her to the ultimate test. Physical labor. Find out once and for all if she's pulling our legs or not."

Elizabeth picking peaches in the hot July sun, battling wasps and ants and fruit flies? Hard to imagine. But what about sweet Beth? Well, yes, he could see Beth happily pitching in where she was needed, cheerfully enduring the annoyances involved in harvesting peaches.

What about your vow to avoid her at all costs? an irritating voice in the back of his mind reminded him.

"So," Hub prompted, "you gonna ask her?"

"I guess so. What choice do I have?"

The harvest came first. He'd just have to rein in his emotions. He could do it. How many times had he hidden his feelings as a child, growing up in the orphanage where his wants and needs never came first. He'd become a master at hiding his own desires.

If he kept his hands and his lips to himself, he could pull it off. No two ways about it, Beth must never guess he was having warm feelings for her.

FLATTERED THAT KURT ASKED HER TO HELP WITH THE peach harvest, Bonnie rose before dawn, eager to get started. She dressed in blue jeans, sneakers, and a pink long-sleeve shirt, then pulled her hair back into a ponytail.

Bubbling with excitement, she hurried downstairs to help Consuelo make breakfast. They chattered like sisters. Consuelo told Bonnie about her plans for the Peach Festival. For the past two years, Consuelo had won a blue ribbon for her peach preserves, and she was determined to triumph again this year.

Standing in the warm, friendly kitchen, marveling at the way the housekeeper had come to accept her over the past few days, Bonnie felt a wonderful happiness settle over her. How on earth could she ever have found this wonderful ranch boring?

"You know something, Elizabeth," Consuelo said, scrambling eggs in an iron skillet while Bonnie slipped wheat bread into the toaster.

"What?" Bonnie smiled.

"I never thought I'd be saying this, but I'm really starting to like you."

Consuelo's words had Bonnie blushing. She ducked her head to hide her embarrassment.

"I mean it," Consuelo insisted. "When Kurt first told me about your amnesia, I just knew it was some underhanded scheme you'd cooked up to hurt him again. I was ready to rip your tonsils out with my bare hands."

"You're a loyal friend."

"Darn right. Kurt gave me a job and a place to stay when I had no place else to go."

"He's a wonderful man."

Consuelo nodded. "The best."

A lump formed in Bonnie's throat. Kurt was so unselfish. For the millionth time, she wondered how she could ever have deliberately betrayed him.

What would happen if she stopped trying to recover her memory? What if she simply let things alone and built a whole new life for herself. Here. With Kurt. The thought sent a thrill rushing through her.

"Kurt has been hurt so much in his life, I feel he deserves an extra special woman. You can imagine my horror when he wound up with you. I mean...the way you used to be."

"I understand," Bonnie said, but it still hurt to be considered such a pariah. "What do you mean about Kurt being hurt?"

"He had a very sad childhood. Like mine. That's why he

took me in. He understood what it was like to be all alone. He grew up in an orphanage where Hub's parents worked as dorm parents."

Bonnie clicked her tongue. "That's so sad."

"Kurt rebelled and ran away. He shoplifted and stole cars. He was arrested several times and almost got sent to a juvenile detention center, but The Threadgills stepped in. They assumed personal responsibility for him, and it made all the difference in the world."

"Kurt was lucky to have them."

"Mr. Threadgill discovered Kurt had a marvelous head for figures and encouraged him to explore his talents. With the help of Hub's parents, Kurt turned his life around. That's why he's so involved with charitable organizations. He translated his wizardry with finances into helping others."

Kurt McNally was a great man. And she didn't deserve him. He was far too good for her. She'd betrayed him, caused him so much pain. It was a tribute to his noble spirit that he'd even allowed her to set foot on his ranch after all the mean things she'd done. But oh, how she wanted him. Wanted him with a desire so deep, so intense, she scarcely dared identify it. And Consuelo's story had only served to intensify her longing.

Bonnie bowed her head and prayed fervently that her memory would never return. She did not want to know the woman she'd once been.

Hub and Kurt showed up for breakfast along with eight peach pickers hired for the harvest. The minute Kurt walked into the room, Bonnie's pulse started pounding. She inhaled in short, rapid gasps, and her hands grew instantly cold despite the heat from the gas oven. Just looking at him had her weak in the knees.

Hub said something that had everyone laughing, and Kurt smiled at his friend, an expression of love shining in his eyes.

A heavy wistfulness rose against her chest like a cruel accusation. Kurt was so full of love for other people, why couldn't he look at her that way too?

Because you were so awful.

Abject misery crawled through her. Could she ever live down the past she could not recall?

Kurt raised his head. Their eyes met.

Suddenly no one else existed. It was just the two of them standing in the kitchen, their gazes joined.

"You look lovely this morning, Beth," Kurt said, moving past the workers crowding into the kitchen. The smell of eggs, sausage, and coffee scented the air.

"Th-thank you," Bonnie said, unnerved by the unabashed appreciation reflected on his face. His pupils dilated as his gaze traveled from the V of her shirt to the tight jeans encasing her hips and thighs.

"Too pretty to be out sweating for peaches."

"I can handle it." She raised her chin. She wasn't about to let him down. This was her chance to prove herself as one of them. She would pick peaches until she dropped.

"It's going to be a busy day."

"I'll survive."

"Are you sure you're up to it? It's only been five days since your accident."

Bonnie touched her bruised temple. "I'm okay."

"If you start to feel lightheaded, I want you to stop right away. Understand?"

"Sure." She smiled and pushed her glasses up on her nose.

"I like those glasses on you."

"Thanks." She glanced at the toasted bread in her hands. "Here," she said, extending the plate toward him. "Let's get this crew fed."

"Spoken like a true farmer's wife."

Wife.

Once the word was uttered, it hung between them like an invisible curtain. Kurt reached for the plate. Their fingers touched.

Bonnie hissed in her breath. Kurt turned quickly and headed for the table. Had he felt it, too? she wondered, this inexplicable stirring deep within his soul?

The hungry farm workers quickly consumed the massive breakfast she and Consuelo had prepared. The housekeeper stayed behind to clean the kitchen while Bonnie followed the men outside.

Dawn stretched across the eastern horizon. Dew clung to grass blades and dampened their shoes as they tramped across the lawn toward the flatbed work trucks loaded with empty bushel baskets. From what Consuelo had told her, Bonnie knew that by evening, every one of those baskets would be brimming with freshly picked fruit.

"Ride with me," Kurt invited before Bonnie could swing into the bed of a truck beside the other harvesters. "I want to talk to you." He took her elbow and guided her over to his Jeep.

Oh gosh, Bonnie fretted. What had she done wrong? "Is something the matter?" she asked timidly, climbing into the passenger seat beside him.

"Not at all." He smiled. Bonnie couldn't help grinning in return. "I just wanted to give you a few pointers on picking peaches." He keyed the engine and started across the pasture, the work trucks lumbering behind them.

"Okay."

She listened attentively as he described the proper way to harvest peaches. The more he talked, the more animated his face became.

He loves this, she thought. Passionately.

Despite his genius for finances, his love of rodeo, and his penchant for championing hard-luck cases, Kurt McNally was, at heart, a farmer. She saw it in the way he cupped his hands when he talked about the ripe peaches, heard it resonate in the timbre of his voice when he spoke of the importance of raising crops to feed the hungry.

His impassioned speech spread goose bumps over her arms. The man was bursting at the seams with love. Love for people, love for plants, love for the land. Love for everything except her.

Bonnie pushed that sad thought from her mind. Kurt might not even like her, but lately he'd been very kind. He smiled more often, asked her opinion, and seemed sincere in his desire to help her regain her memory. Just being here with him was enough. It had to be. She had no idea what tomorrow might bring and no right to plan for the future.

The vehicle's windows were rolled down. The heady aroma of succulent peaches greeted them. Bonnie stuck her head out the window and took a deep breath. It was going to be a glorious day.

He stopped the Jeep, and they got out. The other workers joined them and within minutes were busily picking peaches. Kurt handed Bonnie a pair of gloves to put on. She savored the feel of coarse cotton. The sensation reminded her of gardening.

Gardening.

She experienced a sudden flash of a memory. A garden plot planted behind a small house. Bonnie closed her eyes and raised a hand to her brow. She saw carrots and lettuce and cucumbers, smelled freshly tilled earth, tasted the acid bite of ripe tomatoes.

"Are you okay?" Kurt asked, placing a hand on her shoulder, concern in his voice. "If you're not feeling well, I'll take you back to the house."

"No, no, I'm fine."

"Are you sure?"

"I had a recollection. Like the one in the drugstore."

"Tell me about it," he said.

"I remember a garden."

"Where?"

"Behind a small house. I think I lived there."

Kurt shook his head. "Beth, I don't know what to make of your memories. It seems you're remembering things that never happened. I swear you used to freak out if you even got dirt on your hands. You've never gardened."

"I'm here now, aren't I? Helping you pick peaches."

"That's true, but you've been quite different since the accident."

Bonnie shrugged. "I can't help it. That's what I remember."

"Okay. We'll talk about it later. Right now, we've got a crop to harvest."

They set to work on one fruit-laden tree, twisting the delicate peaches from their branches and settling them into bushel baskets. Sweet sticky juice dripped down their arms, and Bonnie quickly understood why Kurt had told her to wear long sleeves.

Wasps buzzed. Ants trooped over the branches. Fruit flies occasionally landed on her lips and eyelashes. Tree leaves scraped her face.

She brushed away the nuisances and kept working. The temperature was already warm, and the bright sun inching up the sky promised more heat to come, but Bonnie didn't care. She loved the physical labor, adored the prevailing scent of peaches, savored sneaking glances at Kurt.

He looked absolutely magnificent, his concentration focused on the job at hand, his tawny hair brushed back, perspiration glistening on his forehead. She wished this day could last forever. For one sweet tenuous moment in time, she was completely, exquisitely happy.

BETH WORKED AS HARD AS ANY OF THE MEN, KURT noticed. She'd amazed him with her stamina. It had been a record harvest. Kurt's body ached with a special kind of exhaustion brought about by hard work and a job well done.

He felt damned good.

He, Hub, Consuelo, and Beth, all freshly showered, sat on the front porch eating bowls of homemade peach ice cream and breathing in the gathering dusk. The harvesters had left after the huge supper Consuelo fed them.

Fireflies flickered through the cottonwood trees. Crickets sang their twilight song. A slight breeze cooled his heated skin.

Kurt looked over at Beth and admired the soft curve of her breasts beneath her white cotton T-shirt. Her damp hair curled around her shoulders, and those adorable glasses were perched on the end of her petite nose.

What a woman.

Beth had been there for him when he'd needed her. That one unselfish act went a long way to healing the hurt she had inflicted. He firmly believed in giving people a second chance. If *he* hadn't been given an opportunity to turn his life around when he was a teenager, Kurt had no doubt he could have ended up in prison.

What could Beth accomplish with a new lease on life? She was kind, considerate, helpful, vigorous, and cheerful. With those attributes, what *couldn't* she accomplish?

What could they accomplish together? he wondered, working as a team as they had this afternoon, turning a tough task into shared joy.

Hold on, McNally. Be logical. You're making plans for the future with a woman who has no memory. It won't work.

But when Beth smiled at him as she was smiling right now

—her chin dipped down, her eyes angling up at him, the tip of her tongue lightly wetting her lips—Kurt did not care about logic or reason. He forgot about the lies she'd told, the roles she'd acted. He forgot about Grant Lewis and the pain she had put him through.

He could think of nothing but Beth. The smell of her hair, the feel of her skin, the taste of her lips. Incredible.

He wanted her so badly, and yet, he was afraid. Afraid as soon as her memory returned, she'd revert to her old ways. Afraid that if she didn't make a full recovery, she'd want to leave anyway.

Oh, hell, who was he kidding? Kurt was afraid to let himself care about her, terrified that if he did, she'd break him all over again.

Taking a deep breath, Kurt shook his head. He had only one choice. To take each day as it came and have absolutely no expectations. It was the only way he could survive with his heart intact.

❧ 14 ❧

The days following the harvest passed in a flurry of preparation as the whole household geared up for the impending festival.

Consuelo's kitchen smelled constantly of sweet peaches and tangy spices. Bonnie scrubbed jelly jars in hot soapy water and toted pails of peaches from the orchard to the kitchen sink. Hub and Kurt constructed a wooden display stand for selling the peaches at the farmers' market and made arrangements to have the peaches shipped.

Bonnie peeled peaches until her fingers were numb and sticky, but she loved the camaraderie she'd formed with Hub's wife as they worked side by side canning peach preserves, baking peach cobbler, and frying peach fritters.

"I don't want to see another peach until next year," Consuelo groaned at midnight on Friday. Wiping her hands on her apron, she collapsed into one chair and propped her feet in the seat of another.

The kitchen gleamed, clean at last. Rows of canned peaches lined the cupboard. Empty bushel baskets were stacked in the corner. Bonnie poured two glasses of chilled peach nectar and handed one to Consuelo before settling into a chair next to her.

"Thanks."

Bonnie smiled.

"You've been a tremendous help, Elizabeth."

"I tried my best."

"You know, if a year ago someone had told me you'd pitch in like this, I would have laughed myself silly."

"I know."

Consuelo leaned over and patted Bonnie's hand. "I'm glad Kurt brought you home to recover."

Home.

That was the kicker. This wonderful ranch was not her home, and these kind, loving people were not her family. Bonnie swirled the murky liquid in her glass. Would she ever know who she was? The last few days had been so busy, she'd almost forgotten that she didn't belong here.

That thought brought a sharp, swift ache to her heart. No matter how she might pretend otherwise, she was no longer Kurt McNally's fiancée. This was Kurt's ranch, not hers. Consuelo and Hub and Jesse were his friends. She was merely a guest, a visitor with a time limit. Sooner or later, Kurt was bound to ask her to leave.

Kurt.

She couldn't stop thinking about him. The man had invaded her mind and captured her soul.

When she helped Consuelo with the laundry, her fingers caressed his denim jeans. When she got up in the night to visit the bathroom, she hesitated in the hallway, straining to hear his breathing through his closed bedroom door. When she lay alone in her bed, she'd whisper his name over and over and over like a lullaby until she fell into a deep sleep, strangely comforted by the magic of those two words—Kurt McNally.

Even now, a knot of longing wadded in her throat, so bittersweet she wanted to cry.

"Well," Consuelo said, finishing off her peach nectar. "I'm ready for bed. I've got to be up by five a.m. Will you turn out the lights when you go upstairs?"

Bonnie nodded, almost too tired to move. Waving a hand at Consuelo, she closed her eyes and breathed in the heavenly aroma.

She loved this place—this ranch, this kitchen, these people. She loved getting up at dawn and working hard. She wanted to stay here forever, making a home, growing peaches, living a quiet, simple life with Kurt. She was falling in love with him.

But he did not love her. She'd hurt him too much, and although he didn't seem as cold and distrustful as the day he'd brought her home from the hospital, he was still very wary.

Bonnie couldn't blame him. No sensible person would trust her. Things could not continue this way. She had to get her memory back. After the festival was over, she had one alternative—allow Dr. Freely to do more tests on her. The experience might be traumatic, but she had to know. One way or the other, she had to have closure on her past and make peace with what she had been.

Determined, Bonnie got to her feet and made her way out of the kitchen, flicking off lights as she went. Yes. She couldn't move forward, couldn't truly obtain Kurt's forgiveness and hope for a future, until she knew the truth about the woman she'd once been.

Saturday morning brought perfect festival weather. The sun's bright heat was blunted by fluffy clouds and a cooling breeze. By seven o'clock, breakfast had been finished, the dishes washed and put away.

A party atmosphere prevailed as they loaded the vehicles. Hub joked, Kurt whistled, Consuelo smiled. A blue jay chattered from a pecan tree in the front yard. Angus cattle grazed along the fence row. In the flower bed, zinnias swayed.

Bonnie absorbed the nuances, savoring everything. Who knew how long this brief happiness would last? She took full advantage of small pleasures—the sunshine on her face, the scent of morning dew, the taste of peaches lingering on her tongue.

Hugging herself, she wished she could freeze this moment in time.

Kurt came over and laid a hand on her shoulder. "Come with me," he invited.

Was it her imagination or was Kurt's voice unnaturally husky, as if he was extremely nervous?

She looked up at him. His hazel eyes gleamed. His gaze roved over her body, taking in the frilly white ruffled blouse tucked into pale blue jeans. He lingered at her waist before glancing lower. There was no mistaking the message.

Bonnie sucked in her breath, overwhelmed by the arousal written on his face. From that first time he'd kissed her, she had wondered what it would feel like to be made love to by this potent man. Suddenly, she knew if she wanted it, she could maneuver him into her bed.

"Uh...I..." she stammered.

"Hub's taking Consuelo to the administrative tent to enter her preserves in the contest. I've got to deliver peaches to our booth at the farmers' market. Would you like to go with me, or do you prefer to ride with Hub and Consuelo?"

What a question! What she wanted and what was prudent were two very different things.

A thatch of hair flopped across his forehead. Before Bonnie realized what she was going to do, she reached out and brushed the errant lock away. The intimate gesture was possessive, the way a wife might touch her husband.

Kurt's eyes widened. Bonnie's fingers tingled from their

contact. Quickly, she pulled her hand away and took a step backward.

"I...I better ride with Consuelo," she whispered.

His hand snaked out and snared her wrist. "Why?"

Oh my! Bonnie gulped. His fingers seared her skin. "Er, uh, I think it's best."

"Are you afraid to be alone with me?"

Yes! His hold on her wrist was compelling, intoxicating, undeniable.

But she was not afraid of Kurt, rather Bonnie was afraid of her body's own treacherous betrayal. When she was with him, her heart urged her to throw all caution to the wind, to forget her memory loss and the problems that stood between them. Temptation nudged her to court his kisses, to encourage his exploration. Her soul begged her to collapse helplessly into his arms and stay there.

Forever.

Fortunately, her brain knew better.

Before she could make the decision, Hub backed Kurt's Jeep out of the driveway.

"Guess that settles that." Kurt grinned. "You're coming with me."

***

KURT OPENED THE PASSENGER DOOR OF THE BATTERED pickup, then swept his arm and bowed from the waist. Bushel baskets full of peaches lay nestled in the truck bed. Crumpled work gloves and old rags sat in the seat. Kurt brushed the items to the floorboard and waited for Beth to climb inside.

She flicked her hair over her shoulders, and his knees buckled. *Lord above but she was magnificent.*

Kurt's heart rumbled like a drum solo. What in the name

of common sense was he doing? Touching Beth, gazing at her this way, asking her to ride with him.

Alone.

The last thing he needed was to be alone with her when he was having such dangerous thoughts.

But he didn't care who she'd once been or how she had acted. Elizabeth Destiny, the Hollywood actress, was gone and, in her place stood plain, simple Beth. The woman he'd dreamed of his entire life. The woman he'd thought he was getting when he first asked Elizabeth to marry him.

The woman he loved.

Don't be ridiculous, the voice in the back of his mind insisted. How can you love a woman you don't even know?

Indeed, how could he know her when she didn't know herself? Kurt swallowed and shut the pickup door.

Beth stared straight ahead, her chin trembling.

Was she frightened? Or excited? Or both. The thought that she might be as aroused as he had Kurt's breath coming in short spurts.

Down boy, he chided. Much as he desired her, he could not allow his baser instincts to get the better of him.

He scarcely remembered driving into Rascal. What he did remember was Beth's strawberry and cream aroma, her long eyelashes sweeping her cheek as she kept her gaze focused on the floor, her slender hands folded in her lap.

Outside the farmers' market, Kurt backed the truck into an empty parking place and stilled the engine. The open-air stalls were already crowded with vendors. Shading his eyes with his hand against the bright morning sun, Kurt got out.

Beth followed and stood beside the truck. She crossed her arms and anxiously shifted her weight from foot to foot.

Kurt opened the tailgate and tugged out a bushel basket.

"Let me help," she said, coming up behind him.

"I can manage."

He grasped the basket with both arms, and his biceps bulged. It pleased him to note she stared at his muscles. Throwing his shoulders back, Kurt strutted across the asphalt. He just knew she was eyeing his behind. Smiling to himself, he made a show like a peacock preening for a peahen.

He set the basket down at their stall and glanced over his shoulder, eager to see if Beth had appreciated his strength, but she was nowhere in sight.

Huh?

Disappointment arrowed through him. Maybe he'd been wrong. Maybe she wasn't as attracted to him as he'd thought.

Where had she gone? Had another man captured her interest? Feeling jealous, he swiveled his head, surveying the crowd.

Then he saw her helping an elderly lady maneuver her walker over the cracked sidewalk. Immediately, he felt like an idiot. He'd gotten so used to being suspicious of Beth's motives, he almost couldn't believe she would assist someone out of kindness.

Big egotistical jerk, he chided, but part of him was relieved Beth hadn't been admiring someone else. Humbled, he went back to the truck for another basket.

A few minutes later, Beth joined him at the fruit stand.

"I saw you helping that lady," he commented. "That was sweet of you."

Beth waved a hand. "It was nothing."

"Not to you, maybe, but I bet the lady was quite grateful."

"It seemed the thing to do." She shrugged.

The spot of color staining her cheeks had Kurt itching to kiss her. Clearing his throat, he started arranging the peaches into baskets. He'd brought a calculator, paper sacks, and a cash bag for change. Next thing he knew, they were doing an active business. Beth waited on the customers while Kurt handled the money.

Damn, but they made a fine team. From the time he'd been dumped at the orphanage, it was the one thing Kurt had wanted from life that he hadn't achieved. A true helpmate. A woman who worked by his side, to stick with him through thick and thin, to be there, no matter what.

A woman like Beth.

He watched her surreptitiously. The soft material of her white blouse swayed against her slender form as she moved, creating havoc inside him. She greeted each customer as if they were a respected friend, smiling and making small talk. Like children to an ice-cream wagon, people gravitated to her. Folks lingered at their stall, dragging out the conversation. Beth's laughter, light and lilting, filled his ears and warmed his heart.

An hour later, Hub showed up. Greeting them, he tilted his cowboy hat back on his head and leaned his angular body against the stand.

"Hey, Boss, you want me to take over so you two can go see the sights? The parade starts in ten minutes."

"What about Consuelo?"

"She's happy as a kid in a candy store showing off her preserves." Hub grinned wide. "She took first prize again. I tell you, Boss, that woman can cook."

"I know you're proud of her," Beth said, congratulating him.

Hub tipped his cowboy hat back on his head. "You bet I am, little miss."

Kurt looked at Beth. "Would you like to go watch the parade?"

"Sure." The smile she surrendered melted his heart like butter in the broiler.

Leaving Hub to man the stall, Kurt took Beth's arm and guided her through the crowd. They walked past the farmers' market and down the street toward the courthouse. The town square had been cordoned off to vehicular traffic.

Excited children carried brightly colored helium balloons and chewed cotton candy. Harried parents pushed strollers and corralled preschoolers. Folks lined the road, eyes straining for signs of the parade.

Holding Beth's hand, he steered her to a spot on the corner. He loved the way his large palm swallowed her small one. As they traveled through the gathering throng, several people pointed and whispered. Kurt heard the name "Elizabeth Destiny" mentioned more than once. Protectively, he drew her closer to his side.

"The parade will come down North Main." He gestured in that direction.

"Is this the first time I've been to the festival?" Beth asked.

Kurt narrowed his eyes. "You refused to come last year. Said you weren't having anything to do with small-town hicks."

She looked embarrassed.

"Don't feel bad. You're not like that anymore."

"What if I am?" she whispered, and he saw real fear reflected on her face. "What will happen when I get my memory back, Kurt?"

He squeezed her hand. "I don't know."

She shivered, and he encircled her in his arms, drawing her against his chest and burying his nose in her hair. The same fears that haunted her troubled him as well. He wanted to love her, fully, completely, but he couldn't.

Not yet.

Not until her amnesia had been resolved.

And then what? Well, he just didn't know, did he?

"I've been thinking," she said, allowing him to hold her close.

"Uh-huh." He was befuddled by her nearness, his senses overwhelmed.

"I want to go back to Dr. Freely for more testing."

"Are you sure?"

"I...we...can't move forward until this is settled." Briefly, she lifted a hand to her temple. The bruise had almost vanished.

We? Was she seriously considering a future with him?

Before Kurt could explore that provocative thought, the sound of the Rascal High School marching band caught their attention. The music grew louder as the parade proceeded from Main Street to the town square. Tubas blared, drums thundered, and leggy majorettes twirled spangled batons.

"Later," he said, "we'll talk."

She nodded.

Elizabeth was right. Before they could make plans, she had to regain her memory. Until then, they were mired hopelessly in the present, prisoners of the past, uncertain of their future.

Gaily decorated floats followed the band, then came cowboys on well-groomed horses. The Festival Queen drifted by in a convertible, surrounded by her attendants, smiling and waving.

A high school mascot dressed in a pirate costume threw hard candy, whistles, and plastic toys into the crowd. Squealing children scattered to snatch up the goodies.

Kurt took Beth's arm and guided her around the square. They stopped at the various booths, surveyed the wares, and took their luck at games of chance.

Beth glanced at her watch. "Hey, I've got to man the kissing booth at one, and you're due to be dunked at the same time."

"Let's skip out," Kurt growled in her ear.

She swatted him lightly on the shoulder, and that innocent gesture branded him as surely as a fiery kiss. "And disappoint Sarah Jane and Tammy? We can't do that."

"Easy for you to say, you get kissed while I get dumped in a vat of cold water."

"You'll live." Her blue eyes twinkled.

"Not if I have to watch strange men kiss you."

"Jealous?"

"Maybe a little." He held up his thumb and index finger to measure off an inch.

Beth arched her eyebrows. "Hmmm."

"All right, a lot."

She smiled. "Don't worry, no one is going to steal my heart."

"Not even Grant Lewis?"

Once the words were out of his mouth, Kurt could have bitten off his tongue. The teasing light evaporated from her eyes, and her mouth turned down at the corners.

"I suppose I deserved that," she said softly.

"Listen, Beth, I didn't mean it the way it sounded."

"Sure you did." She turned her head away from him. "And you had every right to say it."

He took her chin in his palm and forced her to look at him. The wounded look in her blue eyes cut him to the quick. "No. I have no right to make you feel bad. If I'm going to forgive you for the past, I can't keep throwing it back in your face."

"You're willing to forgive me?" She blinked, obviously incredulous.

"I have to, don't I? If we're going to start fresh."

❦

OH DEAR. HIS WORDS HAD BONNIE EXHALING IN A LARGE whoosh.

"You mean it?" she whispered.

Kurt shrugged. "I can't make any promises, Beth. We have to take every day as it comes."

But the fact he was willing to reconsider their relationship was a vast improvement over the cold way he'd treated her on the day she came home from the hospital. They'd both grown and changed over the course of the last week.

Anxiety gripped her. She had to do something. Soon. Monday morning she'd call Dr. Freely and make an appointment.

"Let's grab something to eat before we have to go man those booths," Kurt said.

Food booths had been constructed on the south side of the square. The scent of hamburgers, fajitas, and barbecue enticed them over. Nudging around the crowd, Kurt paid for their lunch. They found a vacant table on the sidewalk and sat down to watch the people strolling by.

Bonnie absorbed the atmosphere. She loved every minute. The crowd, the noise, the sights and smells. Across the way, a lady was doing face paintings. Down the street, peddlers hawked handmade crafts. On the courthouse lawn, someone was orchestrating a sack race.

Savoring the taste of the fajitas, Bonnie wondered what it would be like to live with Kurt as man and wife. Did she dare hope for such a dream to come true?

She peeked over at him.

His regal profile had her stomach doing flip-flops. Simply looking at the man did crazy things to her. A sultry heaviness settled in her abdomen.

"There you are!" Tammy squealed as she and Sarah Jane bounced over to join Bonnie and Kurt at their table. "Come on, it's time for your turn at the kissing booth. I know you're gonna make tons of money for the courthouse renovations."

"Hey," Sarah Jane said to Bonnie. "I like your glasses. They make you look smart."

"Thanks." Bonnie grinned at the girls.

"Put on fresh lipstick," Tammy advised. "The fellas are going to want lip prints as proof they've been kissed by Elizabeth Destiny."

Bonnie took her compact out of the purse she'd bought when Kurt had taken her shopping and reapplied her lipstick. Puckering, she turned to face Kurt.

He sat with his arms crossed over his chest, scowling. It dawned on Bonnie that her celebrity status bothered him. Was he afraid a taste of the old fame and fanfare would tempt her away from him?

Leaning over, she lightly kissed his cheek and whispered, "It's for charity, honey."

Red lip prints graced his skin, but Kurt did not wipe away her brand. Instead, he pushed back his chair and extended his arm to her.

"Shall we?" he asked.

Giggling, Bonnie linked arms with him, and they followed Sarah Jane and Tammy to the courthouse square.

Elizabeth Destiny's enlarged publicity photograph had been pasted across the front of the kissing booth. A sign urged festivalgoers to come by for a kiss from the Oscar-winning actress between one and two p.m.

Blushing, Bonnie took her place behind the counter with Sarah Jane, while Tammy lead Kurt to the dunking booth directly across the lawn from them. Bonnie watched as Kurt climbed into the rickety contraption and perched on a precarious board extended over a large water tank. Already a half-dozen boys were lined up, tossing baseballs in their hands and grinning wickedly.

"How 'bout a kiss, Ms. Destiny?" A toothless, elderly man extended a five-dollar bill.

Bonnie's eyes widened. This was going to be harder than she thought. Squaring her shoulders, she leaned over and planted a kiss squarely on the man's bald forehead.

"Thank you. I'll cherish this moment forever. I really like your movie acting," he said.

"That's nice of you to say so."

Smiling, the man swaggered off.

Well, if she could brighten an old man's day, perhaps this wasn't so bad after all.

Before the hour was over, she'd reapplied her lipstick forty-two times, and Kurt had taken almost as many spills into the tank. Each time, he came up sputtering and laughing, but he always swung his gaze in her direction. Bonnie waved, egging him on.

At two o'clock, Kurt sloshed over to get her, water dripping from his clothes. "Where's *my* kiss? I certainly earned one getting dunked by the entire Rascal middle school."

"Right here."

Extremely glad to be rescued, she wrapped her arms around his neck and kissed him full on the mouth.

Kurt captured her bottom lip between his teeth, growled low in his throat, and pulled her flush against his soaking wet body. Bonnie didn't care.

"Hey," a man in the crowd exclaimed. "She didn't kiss me like that!"

"You don't look like that young buck does neither," his companion chuckled.

The man wandered off, grumbling.

Kurt broke the kiss and beamed down at her. "Let's go home and change, then we'll relieve Hub at the fruit stand."

"Sure." With Kurt McNally, she would go anywhere.

Hand in hand, they made their way back to the pickup. Bonnie's damp jeans molded to her thighs; the wetness felt good in the afternoon heat.

Kurt's hair was slicked back on his forehead. His shirt was plastered to him, showcasing his muscles. He looked over at her. The gleam in his eyes was purely sexual.

Bonnie shivered as it dawned on her that she and Kurt were going to be completely alone back at the ranch. Stripping off their clothes, taking showers, and getting dressed without Consuelo buzzing around the kitchen. No Jesse running up and down stairs. No Hub to interrupt them if...

She batted away that thought. Much as she wanted Kurt, much as she might want to make love to him, she could not allow herself. Not until her amnesia had been resolved, because Bonnie could not remember ever having made love to this man. She knew she could not give her body to him without giving her whole self—heart, mind, and soul. Yet how could she surrender herself when she didn't know who in the world Elizabeth Destiny truly was?

To Bonnie's disappointment, Kurt was a perfect gentlemen. Not once did he make any sexual overtures. He left her standing in the hallway while he disappeared upstairs and emerged ten minutes later fully dressed.

She fretted about his lack of interest all the way back to the farmers' market. She'd changed into her pink sundress that she had planned to wear to the dance, and she noticed he didn't keep glancing at her cleavage as he had the first time she'd worn it.

Why?

They sold peaches for the rest of the afternoon, and Kurt didn't give the slightest indication that anything was amiss. Had she misread the signals he'd sent her that morning? What about that potent kiss he'd planted on her in the kissing booth? Was he having second thoughts about giving their relationship another chance?

Bonnie pouted. She'd had no intention of being seduced, but the man could have at least tried.

"Hey, sugarplum." He chucked her under the chin. "What's with the long face? I thought you were having a good time?"

"I was. Guess I'm just feeling a little sad." His term of endearment erased some of her fear. If he was upset with her, why the sweet talk?

"What's the matter?" Honest concern in his eyes.

"I'm afraid."

"Of what?"

"Of losing you."

Kurt said nothing. She knew he could offer her no promises. Hadn't expected it.

"We better be going." He cleared his throat. "Hub and Consuelo are waiting."

She nodded, fighting back the lonely ache chilling her straight to her marrow.

When Consuelo showed up, they all piled into Hub's car and drove over to the Sheriff's Posse arena where the Food and Wine Festival dance was held.

After paying to park, Hub circled the dirt area before finally spotting an empty space. A live band played a country and western tune, the plaintive guitar twanging into the gathering twilight. Mouthwatering aromas wafted on the breeze from the pit barbecue set up behind the parking area.

They walked toward the purple tent sheltering a cement dance floor. People milled around, laughing, joking, clapping their hands in time to the music. Children played tag. Dogs chased each other. Teenagers lolled against their cars, trying to look cool.

Bonnie tried to shake her wistful mood. She should be in seventh heaven. What more could she ask for? Pleasant weather, good friends, great music, delicious food, a handsome man by her side.

The only thing missing was her memory.

"You okay?" Kurt asked.

"Fine." She gave him a wan smile. She should be happy. If nothing else, this bout with amnesia had taught her to enjoy each moment.

"Tired? Want to go home?"

Home. To the ranch. But that was the problem. The ranch was not her home. She didn't know where she belonged.

"Beth?" Kurt stopped.

Consuelo and Hub walked on.

He drew her protectively into the circle of his arm. Bonnie breathed in his fresh, outdoorsy scent. God, she loved him so much. Was it possible she had once committed the ultimate betrayal against him? And still, despite the pain, despite his reservations, he'd been willing to forgive her.

She didn't deserve him.

A sick feeling roiled in the pit of her stomach. She was trapped in a catch-22. If her memory never returned, how could she hope to give herself to him fully, freely? And if she did remember, wouldn't she then revert to the awful person she'd once been and thereby betray him all over again?

Bonnie clenched her fists. No. She would not put Kurt through additional misery. Better she suffer than he. She would leave him forever before she would do that.

"Cheer up. Things will get better, I promise." His smile was so sweet, so kind, Bonnie found herself fighting back tears.

"Let's dance," he said softly, guiding her around folks lined up for the barbecue. "I want to hold you close."

Her heart sped up at his suggestion. Helplessly, she allowed him to lead her into the tent packed with dancers.

"I don't remember how to dance." She balked.

"It's like riding a bicycle. You never forget."

She hung back. "Maybe I never knew how."

"Nonsense. We've danced before."

"But not to country and western music, right?"

Kurt led her gently forward. "Put one hand here." He took her hand and placed it on his shoulder. He wrapped one arm around her waist. "Now, give me your other hand."

She did as she was told. Lacing their fingers together, he swirled her onto the dance floor. The band played a slow, sad ballad.

"That's it," he whispered.

She drifted along, swept away with the magic of his touch. She felt like Cinderella waltzing with Prince Charming. She could scarcely believe her good fortune, but she knew it couldn't last. Except, instead of fearing midnight as Cinderella did, she was terrorized by the thought of getting her memory back. And when her memory returned, would she discover she wasn't the sweet Cinderella, but rather one of the wicked stepsisters?

Enjoy the moment, the voice in the back of her mind insisted.

Bonnie rested her head on Kurt's shoulder and tried not to think. Rather she focused on appreciating him as they swayed together. His thigh brushed hers. His chest grazed her breast. She heard his heart pound, listened to his raspy breathing.

Closing her eyes, she savored the sensation, freezing it in time, forever holding the memory close.

"Maybe this wasn't such a good idea," he said gruffly.

Raising her head, she opened her eyes, meeting his steady gaze.

"What do you mean?"

"Dancing with you, holding you like this, is driving me crazy. I want to get you alone."

"Kurt!" she said, shocked.

"Do I embarrass you?"

She ducked her head.

"Desire is nothing to be ashamed of."

"I'm confused."

"Of course you are. I am, too. If last Friday someone had told me I'd be talking to you like this, I would have told them to get a reality check. But you've convinced me, Beth. You have done a complete one-eighty turnaround."

She darted him a quick glance. "Aren't you afraid I'll change back when my memory returns?"

He shook his head. "I think the changes in you are permanent."

"What if they're not?"

His Adam's apple bobbed when he swallowed. His forehead wrinkled. "For you, Beth, I'm willing to take that risk."

"Knowing how much I've hurt you in the past? You'd really forgive me to that extent?"

"How can I not?" he whispered.

"No." She pulled away from him and bumped into another couple. Mumbling her apology, she streaked across the dance floor and out of the tent, her chest heaving.

"Beth!" Kurt's footsteps echoed behind her. "Wait."

She stopped and looked up at the stars. Blood rushed through her ears with each heartbeat. The cool night breeze raised the hairs on her arm, and Bonnie shivered.

"Don't run from me."

Holding up her palms, she stepped backward. "Please, Kurt. Much as I'd like to, I can't promise anything. Not now. Not as long as I'm living in limbo. It wouldn't be fair to you."

"Before the accident, you wouldn't have cared about treating me fairly." He reached out and fingered the strap of her sundress. That simple gesture told her just how vulnerable he was feeling. How badly she must have hurt him!

"I care now. Let me see Dr. Freely again and see what she says."

Kurt stuck his hands into his pockets. "You're probably right."

"Hey, you two." Hub sauntered over, oblivious to the tension between them. "The sliced barbecue sandwiches are great if you're hungry."

"Huh?" Kurt blinked.

Relieved to be distracted, Bonnie turned to Consuelo and congratulated her on winning the blue ribbon for her peach preserves. For the rest of the evening, she avoided Kurt as much as possible, and he didn't seek her out again.

By the time they got back to the ranch, Bonnie was so restless, she knew she wouldn't be able to sleep. Her mind whirled with crazy, irrational hope. Could Kurt truly be hers? Would she even want him when her memory returned?

"Good night," Kurt said outside her bedroom door. He looked as confused as she felt.

"Good night."

Neither moved.

They heard Hub and Consuelo downstairs. Kurt nervously snapped his fingers.

Bonnie raised an eyebrow. "Yes?"

"Nothing."

But he did want to say something. She could see it in the set of his shoulders, the tilt of his mouth.

"Good night," he repeated, but this time he turned on his heels and headed into his own bedroom.

Bonnie fought the urge to follow him as she closed her door behind her and collapsed onto the bed. Finally, she'd convinced Kurt that she was not the old Elizabeth. After more than a week, he'd come to believe in her again. He'd wanted to make love to her. But this time, she'd been the one to call a halt. She could not make love to him. Not until she knew for sure what the future held.

Miserable, she changed into a thin, white cotton nightgown and slipped between the sheets. She closed her eyes and willed sleep to overtake her.

No such luck. Images of Kurt played relentlessly against the back of her eyelids.

Kurt demonstrating how to pick peaches. His T-shirt clinging to his muscular biceps, looking for all the world like a Greek god beamed down to earth for her express pleasure.

Kurt reluctant and stern, but arriving at the hospital nonetheless, rescuing her despite the anguish she'd caused him.

Kurt wet from the dunking booth, his hair slicked back, smiling good-naturedly and gathering her to his chest in a bear hug.

Kurt lingering outside her bedroom door, waiting on her, wanting her.

Bonnie's eyes flew open, and she threw back the covers. This wouldn't do. She had to get some fresh air, clear her mind and try to think. If only she could trigger her memory. If only she could find out why she had behaved as she did. If only she could find some answers.

Slipping into her shoes, she padded to the landing. She stood there a moment, listening. The house was silent. On tiptoes, she stole downstairs.

She let herself out the front door. A warm breeze stirred, whipping her nightgown around her legs as she trotted down the path. A three-quarters moon rested in the sky, lighting her way.

Peach trees, stripped of fruit, waved their branches at her as she stumbled past the orchard. She'd forgotten her glasses, but she didn't care. Bonnie didn't even know where she was headed. She just knew she had to walk, to move, to jolt her sluggish memory.

She followed the fence row and climbed a small hill. Tall grass slapped at her knees, itching her skin. When she reached the top of the rise, she found herself staring down at a small lake shimmering silver in the darkness.

The lake where Kurt told her he had proposed.

Bonnie swallowed. If any place could make her remember, this would be it.

Carefully, she picked her way to the edge of the lake. Her shoes made imprints in the moist earth. The darkness did not frighten her. In fact, she found the anonymity welcoming.

A whippoorwill called to her. An owl answered. A light mist covered the water. She paused beneath a weeping willow, its slender branches waving against her in the wind like ghostly fingers.

Spying a large, flat rock, Bonnie sat down, hugged her knees to her chest, and stared out over the murky water.

Was she Elizabeth Destiny, the brittle, hard-hearted actress who desired fame and fortune at all costs, or was she Beth, the woman who wanted Kurt McNally and life on the ranch?

"Or am I someone else entirely?" she whispered.

Her head ached with the effort of sorting the mess her life had become. As Elizabeth Destiny, she might have been a cold-blooded witch, but at least she had been sure of herself.

Bonnie rubbed her temple and sighed. She felt so frustrated, so confused. Too bad she'd have to wait until Monday to see Dr. Freely. She'd grasp at any remedy, any chance for answers. Anything was preferable than this uncertainty.

Resting her cheek against her knee, she sighed and thought of Kurt.

A twig snapped.

Frightened, Bonnie swiveled her head. Her pulse quickened in response.

Through the mist she saw a shadowy form. *Oh my gosh. I've come out alone in the dead of night without considering my safety.* Prepared to run, Bonnie lifted a hand to her chest.

"Beth?" Kurt's voice, low and calm, floated from the darkness, folding around her like protective armor.

Relief flooded her body. Her legs felt strangely weak. "Yes?"

"I was worried about you." Parting the willow's feathery limbs, he moved closer, his features cloaked.

"I'm okay."

"Are you?"

She wanted to say yes, that she was fine, and he shouldn't fret over her. Instead a sudden sob bubbled up inside her and burst from her lips.

"Sugarplum?" In a second, he was beside her, one strong arm sliding around her waist.

She buried her head against his chest, her shoulders shaking.

"Tell me," he coaxed, gently stroking her head.

"I...can't," she gulped.

"Sure you can. It's me, Kurt. We used to be engaged. Remember?"

"No," Bonnie wailed. "That's the problem. I don't remember."

"Shh." He rocked her back and forth like a baby, then planted a light kiss on her forehead.

Nothing had ever felt so good. For a moment, Bonnie allowed herself to cherish his kiss.

"I'm here for you. Whenever you're ready to talk."

She didn't deserve this, his tender caring. How desperately she wanted to confess her feelings. But Bonnie didn't dare. She refused to hurt him again.

Kurt hugged her tighter. She breathed in his smell—woodsy, natural, honest. Just like the man. His starched denim shirt crinkled, the material contrasting sharply against her thin cotton nightgown.

If she were smart, she would hop up and put as much distance between them as she could, but Bonnie's legs seemed to have melted into the cool stone beneath them. It felt much too good, held safe in his arms. Here, she didn't have to think, didn't have to worry about tomorrow.

"Beth." Kurt shifted his weight, but kept his arm firmly around her waist, his fingers resting just below her ribs. The sensation drove spikes of longing straight through her bones. "I want you so much."

She squirmed. "No, Kurt. We...I...can't. How can I give myself to you when I don't know who I am. You don't understand."

"I want you more than I ever thought possible."

"You don't know what you're saying," she said.

"Yes, I do. You're the one who tolerated my rude behavior. You're the one who played the piano at church when no one else would. You pitched in and helped with the peach harvest when we needed it the most. You won over Consuelo and even Hub. You befriended Tammy and Sarah Jane. You're a good person, Beth." He took her hand in his and squeezed.

Her resolve to keep him at arm's length dissolved like snowflakes on a hot grill.

Gently, Kurt eased her into his lap, his thigh muscles knotted brick-hard beneath her bottom. "I know you're confused but that's understandable. I want to help you through this. Will you let me, Beth?"

"Yes," she whispered, wrapping her arms around his neck and indulging in her storybook fantasy of happily ever after. Maybe things could work out between them. Hope lifted her heart like eagles' wings.

LORI WILDE

"I want to kiss you," he announced.

Her stomach fluttered. She gazed into his eyes and found herself falling into a wondrous abyss. Hungrily, eagerly, his lips closed over hers. Bonnie breathed in his taste. Minty, sweet, perfect.

"Oh, Kurt." She sighed.

He laced his fingers through her hair, pulled her closer, kissed her deeper.

Bonnie knew this wasn't the right time to surrender herself to Kurt, but she couldn't fight the overwhelming desire his kisses ignited. Her nipples hardened, straining against her nightgown. Her lower abdomen grew heavy with longing. Her toes curled in pure delight.

"You do dangerous things to me, Beth."

"Me? Dangerous?"

"Deadly." He nodded, breaking their kiss and leaning back to look at her. "You take my breath."

She giggled, and her hair fell across her face.

Kurt lifted his hand and reached for the button on her nightgown. Hesitating, he raised an eyebrow. "Do I go further?"

Bonnie knew she should shout no! but instead found herself whispering, "Yes."

Awkwardly, he undid three small buttons and pushed the cloth aside, revealing the top of her breasts. Lowering his head, he imprinted kisses down her neck, his mouth slowly traveling south. His hands cupped her soft flesh.

"You taste so good," he groaned.

"So do you."

"Not as good as you. When I kiss your skin, I think of strawberry shortcake with mounds of whipped cream."

She giggled again. "Then kiss me again."

Stop.

TO KURT, THE SOUND WAS PURE MAGIC. HE COULDN'T believe his luck. To get Elizabeth back the way he had always dreamed she could be. Kind, lovable, considerate. Beautiful.

Seven weeks ago when he caught Elizabeth in bed with Grant, his life had been in shambles, and now he felt as if he'd been gifted with the keys to heaven. Heaven that smelled and tasted and sounded like this sweet angel.

With Beth clutched tightly in his arms, he rolled them off the rock in one smooth motion. They collapsed laughing into the short, damp grass beside the lake. Moonlight reflected off her face, highlighting her slender nose, that petite chin. Her eyes widened as she stared up at him.

"I want you. Here. Now."

Beth whimpered and nodded her approval.

"Anytime you want me to stop, just say so."

"Don't stop."

He grinned and lowered his head. His hands roamed over her body, kneading her buttocks, tickling her waist, teasing her breasts with his mouth through the thin cotton.

She wriggled, urging him on.

He raised himself on one elbow and undid the rest of the pearly buttons on her nightgown. He curled back the restraining material, his eyes taking in the feast before him.

Kurt had been against Elizabeth having a breast augmentation, but she'd insisted she needed to have it done for her career. She'd gone from a B cup to a D. He looked down at her exposed chest and blinked.

Something wasn't right. Something that had been nagging him from the moment he picked Beth up at the hospital. Her breasts weren't as big as they once were. They were very nice. Round, firm, and not too small, but after surgery, her breasts had been much larger.

Staring, he stopped touching her and sat up.

"What's the matter?" Beth asked, covering herself with her hands. "Did I do something wrong?"

An odd sensation shuddered through Kurt. How had Elizabeth's artificial breasts gotten smaller? Had she had them removed? But when?

"What's going on here?" he demanded.

"I don't know what you mean." Alarm skewed her face.

"Did you have more surgery?" he rasped, a sharp spike of pain wedging deep inside his gut.

Beth shook her head. "No."

Oh, Lord, Kurt thought, please let me be wrong about her. But in his heart, he knew!

Even now, with anger spurting through his veins, he wanted her. Desired her more than he ever had any woman. The hard tightness below his belt was proof of that. He had to get to the bottom of this.

"Elizabeth," he said harshly. "What are you trying to pull?"

"Nothing!" Her voice rose, high and hysterical.

He raked his gaze over those beautiful breasts, leaning close for a better view. If she'd had them reduced, the scars would be fresh. It was only seven weeks since they'd broken up. Except there were no scars.

No scars at all.

What did this mean? She'd had her breasts augmented. There had been scars before. Well concealed scars for sure, she'd had a top-notch plastic surgeon, but scars nonetheless.

"Damn!" Kurt shoved her aside and staggered to his feet, his breath coming in sharp, ragged gulps. Not again! He simply could not believe his gullibility.

Who in the hell was this woman?

"What? What's wrong?" Beth, or whoever she was, cried out.

"Oh, don't you dare give me those tears. I'm tired of falling for that." He raked his palm across his mouth, desperate to rid himself of her taste, a terrible queasiness assailing him. His heart pounded blood to his ears as his mind tried to make sense of this charade. If she wasn't Elizabeth, who was she and why was she playing him like a fiddle?

She sat up on her knees, raising her hands to him beseechingly. "Please, tell me what I did wrong."

Disgusted, Kurt turned his head. "Your first mistake was agreeing to impersonate Elizabeth Destiny."

"I...I..." Beth bit down on her knuckles, her face blanched pale, her hair a blond halo around her. She still looked like an angel, sweet and tempting, but now he knew she'd been sent by the devil, not heaven.

He didn't know why, but Elizabeth was using this look alike to screw with his head.

"I can't believe I fell for it!" Even finding Elizabeth in bed with Grant Lewis hadn't hurt this much.

The woman, whomever she was, stayed on the ground, staring at him, her whole body trembling.

Kurt began to pace. "What an idiot I am. I should have figured it out before now."

"Figured out what?"

"Oh sure, I noticed little things, but not enough to get through my thick skull. You're more delicate and your features more refined, but you're a dead ringer for her."

"Wh...what?" She splayed her right hand across her chest.

"You can stop pretending. I'm onto you."

"I'm not pretending," she wailed. "I really don't know who I am!"

"Damn!" Bending over, he picked up a stone and plunked it into the water with a loud splash. "Your vision problems. Playing the piano. It all makes sense now. You really wrapped me around your little finger. You're a pro. God, what a fool I am." Kurt smacked his forehead with his palm.

"I really *do* have amnesia."

He grabbed the front of her gown in his hands, tugged her to her feet, and shoved his face in hers.

She cringed and tried to pull away.

"How did you fake the accident? How did you fool the doctors? How much did she pay you? Tell me."

Huge, wet tears rolled down her cheeks. Kurt almost felt sorry for her, then he reminded himself this woman had connived with Elizabeth. This woman had hurt him far more deeply than Elizabeth ever could have because he had truly fallen for *this* woman.

"What did you hope to gain?" he demanded.

"I don't know what you're talking about."

"Money? Publicity? A reconciliation?"

"You're acting crazy."

"Damn right. You've driving me crazy! I see the plan now." He smacked his fist into his palm.

"There was no plan."

"Elizabeth calls central casting and tells them to find her a double. Then you two set up the accident. Your job is to get on my good side so she can waltz back in later after I've fallen for you. That's the truth. Admit it! It's exactly something like Elizabeth would do."

"No."

"I have to hand it to you, whoever you are. You're a better actress than Elizabeth, hands down."

"I wasn't acting!"

His face twitched. "Not even when you were kissing me?"

"Especially not then."

"So you admit it, you were acting some of the time."

"No," she moaned and clasped her hands over her ears. "You're twisting my words."

"Hub knew something wasn't right from the start. Jeez, why didn't I listen to him? Why did I trust you?"

"Please, Kurt, think rationally. What you're saying makes no sense."

"Get out of my sight," he said hoarsely.

"Don't do this to me. Please, I'm confused. If I'm not Elizabeth Destiny, who am I?" She reached out to him, her expression beseeching him to listen.

"What the hell do I care?" Kurt said coldly, then turned on his heels and disappeared into the darkness, his heart cracking right in two.

❧ 16 ❦

Emotional pain, excruciating and relentless, drove Bonnie. Blindly, she stumbled back to the house, Kurt's ugly words ringing in her ears.

What the hell do I care?

The cold expression in his eyes had frozen her soul. He hated her. Just as he had the day he'd picked her up at the hospital. Except this was worse. Much worse. Because over the course of the past week, she'd come to see how loving Kurt could be. In one startling moment, his tender feelings had dissolved into black contempt.

Gulping, Bonnie thundered up the stairs, crashed into her bedroom, and slammed the door behind her. Her fingers trembled as she pulled open dresser drawers and stuffed her meager belongings into a garbage sack. Tears streamed down her cheeks in torrents.

She caught sight of herself in the mirror. Her nightgown was buttoned crookedly; her eyes were swollen and red, her hair tumbling in wild disarray.

"Who are you?" Bonnie demanded, stepping closer to the

mirror. "If you're not Elizabeth Destiny, who in the world are you?"

She stared but the pitiful creature reflected there offered no explanation.

"Damn you," she cried, caught up in the utter grief ripping through her. Retrieving a shoe from the floor, Bonnie hurled it at the mirror.

Glass shattered.

Shattered like her dreams, like her heart.

"Elizabeth?" Consuelo tapped at her door. "Are you all right?"

Stepping around broken glass, Bonnie moved to fling open the door. A deep frown marred Consuelo's forehead as she peeped around Bonnie to peer at the carnage on the floor.

"Can you drive me to the bus station in Rascal?"

"Uh...did you and Kurt have a fight?"

"Can you drive me to the bus station?" Bonnie repeated. "And loan me money for a ticket?"

"Yes. I guess so."

"Thank you." Bonnie scooped up the paper bag with her clothing tucked inside. "Can we go now?"

"Let me tell Hub."

Bonnie rested a hand on Consuelo's shoulder. "I'd rather you didn't."

"Elizabeth, what's going on?"

"I don't want to talk about it."

Consuelo blew out her breath. "Okay. I'll get the keys. Are you going to change?"

"Oh." Dazed, Bonnie stared down at her nightgown. "Yeah."

Consuelo brought the car around while Bonnie hastily changed into jeans and a T-shirt. Thumping down the hall, she stopped outside Kurt's bedroom. She doubted he was in there, but it didn't matter. She could still see the anger in his hazel eyes, could still hear his accusation ringing in her ears. Dear Lord, the pain was almost more than she could bear. Sucking back a sob, she fled.

The car dinged because the dome light was one as Bonnie crawled into the passenger seat next to Consuelo. Despite the warm evening, she felt chilled to the bone. Her fingers were pale, bloodless. Shivering, Bonnie hugged herself.

The housekeeper drove toward the highway. "You want to talk about it?" Consuelo briefly touched her shoulder, a note of sympathy in her voice.

Bonnie turned her head and stared into the darkness slipping past the window. She needed someone to confide in. Someone to help her make sense of this horrid mess.

"I'm not Elizabeth Destiny," she whispered.

"I started to suspect you were someone else," Consuelo replied matter-of-factly.

Startled, Bonnie whipped around to look at Consuelo. "How did you know? I didn't even know."

"Elizabeth Destiny is a creep. Even if she had amnesia, it wouldn't have changed her to such an extent that she would have become someone like you."

"Why didn't you say something to Kurt?"

"What was I supposed to say? Hey, Kurt, I don't think this great girl is who you think she is? I figured he'd discover it on his own."

"He did," Bonnie said gruffly, remembering the shock on Kurt's face when he'd examined her breasts. "But he thinks I concocted a plot with Elizabeth."

"For what reason?"

Bonnie shrugged. "To get her back in his good graces, I guess."

"Why does he think Elizabeth would do that?"

"Money, publicity, who knows?"

"That doesn't make sense. Elizabeth has all the money and PR she needs."

"Tell him that."

"Hang in there. Kurt will realize how skewed his thinking is. I'm sure he's very confused and upset."

"Like I'm not!"

"Give him some time to adjust."

"No." Bonnie shook her head vigorously. "You didn't see him. You didn't hear the awful things he said. He'll never forgive me."

"Sure he will. He's just hurting right now. Kurt has an infinite capacity to love. He was even willing to forgive when he thought you were Elizabeth. He's a fair man, and he never stays angry for long."

Consuelo's words were encouraging, but Bonnie knew she couldn't pin her hopes on such tenuous threads. And even if it were true, how could she build something with Kurt when she didn't even know her own name? When she was an enigma to herself?

"Where will you go?" Consuelo asked.

"To San Antonio."

"Where will you stay?"

Bonnie said nothing. She hadn't thought beyond escaping the ranch and Kurt's disdain.

"Do you have money for a hotel?"

"No."

One palm on the steering wheel, Consuelo fished around in her purse with her other hand. She extracted ten twenties from her wallet and extended them to Bonnie.

"I can't—"

"Take it." Consuelo shook the bills at her.

Bonnie stared at the cash. She didn't even have bus fare. What choice did she have?

"I'll pay you back."

"All right."

"You don't know how much I appreciate this." Bonnie folded the money into her pocket.

"Yes, I do. I've been up against it myself." Consuelo flashed her a smile.

A lump rose in Bonnie's throat. "Thank you," she whispered, "thank you for being my friend."

"Here we are," Consuelo said, stilling the engine at the bus stop. "Good luck finding yourself."

"Thank you," Bonnie repeated and for a brief moment, she didn't feel so all alone.

❧

KURT PACED AND WHEELED AROUND THE BARN, HIS BOOTS kicking up dust and bits of hay. One minute his hands were clutched behind his back, the next he was raking his fingers through his hair.

Damn, damn, damn. Was there a bigger fool on the planet earth?

What he felt now was a million times worse than the way he had felt the night he discovered Elizabeth in bed with Grant Lewis. Scratch that, it was a billion times worse. Because that night, a part of him had been relieved at an excuse to break their engagement.

Tonight was a different story.

Tonight he'd been ready to surrender everything.

Tonight he'd experienced a profound stirring deep in his soul when he'd held Beth in his arms. A stirring unlike anything he'd ever experienced before. *This* had been true love.

True love? Ha! How could he be in love with a woman whose real name he did not even know?

Yet her name had nothing to do with that soft, generous light in her blue eyes. A name did not affect the way she'd looked at him, so welcoming, so trusting. Mere nomenclature could not define the essence of that woman who'd changed his life in such a short time. Changed him from a cynic burned by love into a man willing to take another chance.

And it had all blown up in his face. Again.

Face facts, McNally, you're just not destined to find love. You've been blessed with money and success. Let it be enough. You can't have it all.

Standing there in the middle of the barn, bland-faced cattle staring at him, Kurt felt his dreams disappear, slipping through his fingers swifter than sand through an hourglass. Dreams of a wife, children, and happily ever after. Since when did fairy tales come true?

But something obstinate inside him refused to relinquish the dream that had driven him to make money, to support charities, to help others. He'd done it all for the possibility of love.

Love of the woman he knew as Beth.

Beth.

Who was she? Had she conspired with Elizabeth Destiny to trick him? Or was she a hapless victim? Had he jumped to conclusions?

When he'd accused her of treachery, she'd looked so shocked and upset. He'd thought it an act, but now, he wasn't so sure. Part of him wanted so much to believe in Beth's innocence. Because if Beth was innocent, there was hope.

Sudden doubt flickered through him.

Could she really have amnesia and all this was a bizarre case of mistaken identity? The woman *was* the spitting image of Elizabeth Destiny.

Kurt groaned and leaned his head against a stall.

He saw her in his mind's eye, her soft lips trembling, her delicate nose flaring, damp tears trailing down her cheeks. He'd lashed out at Beth, cruelly, blindly, seeking to hurt her the way he'd been hurt. In that moment, he knew he'd done her a grave injustice.

"McNally, what have you done?" he spoke out loud, his words echoing in the big barn.

He had to find Beth. To talk to her and clear up this mess. And if he was wrong, he'd go down on his knees and beg her forgiveness.

"Beth," he called, because he didn't know what else to call her. He flew from the barn; his boots rambled over the dirt as he ran into the darkness, and his heart pounded as if it might leap from his chest.

The lights in the kitchen were on. Kurt banged in through the back door to find Hub and Consuelo sitting at the table.

"Where is she?" he blurted.

"Consuelo took her to the bus station," Hub answered softly. "Looks like you messed up on this one, Boss."

Urgently, Kurt grasped Consuelo's shoulder. "Where was she heading?"

"San Antonio."

"But she has no money. Where was she going to stay?"

"I gave her two hundred dollars. It was all I had on me," Consuelo said.

"How long ago?" Mentally, he was racing ahead, trying to intercept the bus.

"An hour."

"Damn." He could see her, wandering through downtown San Antonio, lost and alone, seeking her identity. And he was the one who'd turned her out in the cold. He, Kurt McNally, the man renowned for helping others. "I've got to find her."

"Boss," Hub said quietly, "it's two o'clock in the morning."

"I don't care. I've got to find her. Now. Tonight. Hub, I think I've made the biggest mistake of my life."

"You are getting very relaxed. That's it. Allow your eyes to close naturally."

Bonnie's eyelids fluttered closed. She tried to relax, but she felt so anxious. Would this work? Would she soon find out who she really was? The thought was terrifying and exhilarating.

"Take a deep breath in through your nose. That's it. Hold it to the count of four. One, two, three, four."

Bonnie did as the hypnotist suggested. She had been afraid to go back to Dr. Freely. Afraid that Kurt might try to trace her through the neurologist. The last thing she wanted was to see that man again. She had one goal—to get her memory back, resume her life, and forget she'd ever heard of Kurt McNally. For the last day and a half, she'd hidden out in a cheap motel, spending the last of Consuelo's money on the hypnotist. If this didn't work, she had no idea where she'd stay tonight.

"You are going deeper and deeper into a state of relaxation." The man's voice droned.

Concentrate, she told herself. *This isn't going to work if you don't cooperate.* Determined, Bonnie focused her attention on taking slow, deep breaths.

Soon, she felt light and airy as if drifting along in a swift stream. Her skin tingled.

"Okay." The hypnotist's voice was low, soothing. "Let's go back. Back to the accident ten days ago."

Eyes closed, Bonnie led her mind back to that afternoon.

"What do you remember?"

"Lying on the pavement. My head hurt," she said. Her tongue felt slow and thick.

"Before that. Think now. What do you remember?"

Bonnie frowned; her body felt so heavy, and she couldn't have opened her eyes if she tried. "Darkness."

"Look beyond the darkness. What do you see?"

"Watch out!" she cried and thrashed her arms.

"What is it? What do you see?"

"A board. Falling."

"Good. Very good. Take a deep breath. That's it."

She could see the board, dangling from some scaffolding. She'd taken off her glasses and slipped them into her purse, but she'd still been able to see that board. Why had she removed her glasses?

"Now," the hypnotist encouraged, "before you walked under the scaffolding, where had you been?"

She shook her head.

"Think. Concentrate. Look at the board, then walk backward."

The scaffolding was erected outside the Federal Building. She recognized that. But who was she and why was she there?

Work. She'd been at work.

"I work downtown," Bonnie said, her voice coming out in a strange monotone.

"Excellent. Take another deep breath. That's right. Let's try a little harder. Can you see where you work?"

"Office. Big office."

"Do you see anyone you know?"

Suddenly, Kurt's face buoyed into her mind. Bonnie shook her head.

"Concentrate," the hypnotist said.

Erasing Kurt's image was easier said than done. Despite her strong desire to know the truth about herself, she kept seeing his tawny hair curling around his ears, kept smelling his unique scent of peaches and sunshine, kept hearing his voice saying those spiteful words, accusing her of things she'd never done.

Or had she?

"Concentrate. You're downtown. In an office. What kind of office?"

Bonnie shook her head, dispelling Kurt at last. Mentally, she looked around the office. "Law office. Briggs, Harrington and Avis."

"Very good." The hypnotist clapped his hands. "What do you do there? Are you a lawyer?"

Bonnie "saw" her computer and the movie memorabilia that cluttered her desk. "No."

"What do you do?"

And then it hit her in a blinding rush. That Friday afternoon in the office. Paige inviting her to go to the *Fast Lane*. The two of them scrolling through the TMZ website. Reading the article about Elizabeth Destiny and Kurt's breakup. Seeing their pictures on the screen.

Bonnie's eyes flew open. "I'm a legal secretary," she shouted. "My name is Bonnie Bradford, and I've never, ever met Elizabeth Destiny in my entire life!"

❦ 17 ❦

"I've got to find her, Hub."

"You'll find her." His friend sounded too calm.

"How? San Antonio has over a million people," Kurt fretted, "how am I supposed to find one Jane Doe? I have no idea where to start."

"You'll figure out something."

Two days had passed since *she,* whoever *she* was, had left the ranch. Two days of pure torture as Kurt had relived each ugly word he'd spoken to her. Two days of driving aimlessly around San Antonio searching for her.

He'd tried Dr. Freely, but had no luck. The doctor hadn't heard from her. He'd cruised the block where Beth had her accident at least a thousand times, desperately scanning the crowded sidewalks for any signs of her.

"Who are you?" he'd mumbled over and over again. "Where are you?" And then to himself, he'd added, *I love you.*

Why had he acted like such a fool when he'd discovered she wasn't Elizabeth Destiny? Why had he allowed fear and suspicion to rule his heart? He should have been thanking his lucky stars she wasn't Elizabeth instead of accusing her of underhanded tactics.

"I'm crazy about her, Hub," he said.

Kurt's chest tightened as he spoke. They were sitting in his business office in downtown San Antonio. Kurt pushed back the miniblinds and stared down at the parking lot below, his stomach churning miserably, his eyes searching the crowd below.

Searching desperately for Beth.

"I know, Boss."

"When I first started dating Elizabeth, I thought I was in love, then she betrayed me, and I realized what an idiot I had been, mistaking lust for love."

Hub nodded and leaned back in his chair.

"I was afraid to trust her again. Even when I knew she wasn't acting. Deep down, I couldn't let go of my fear. I suppose it relates back to my childhood, to being abandoned."

"Yup."

"But this thing I feel for Beth... It transcends anything I've ever experienced."

"Been there. Done that." Hub smiled slightly. "I feel the same way about Consuelo. She's my life, Boss."

"So you understand why I must find her?"

"Any man who's ever loved a woman understands."

"What am I going to do?" Kurt sank onto the edge of his desk and stared at his friend.

"She's your Cinderella, right?"

"Yeah." Kurt grinned at the image. "I guess she is."

"Then take a cue from Prince Charming."

"What are you talking about?"

"He tried the glass slipper on every eligible woman in the county."

"Care to explain yourself?"

"How did Prince Charming let the women know he was on a search?"

Kurt shrugged. "I don't know? How?"

"He advertised."

"Huh?"

Hub held up an index finger. "Take out a Facebook ad. Facebook is really good at hitting a target audience."

Kurt stroked his jaw. "You just might have something there."

Hub made L's with each of his hands and held them out in front of him as if he were framing headlines. "I can see it now. *Cinderella, Where Are You?*"

"Perfect." Kurt snapped his fingers. "I'm going to do it."

Hub grinned. "Ain't love grand?"

"BONNIE, LOOK AT THIS!" PAIGE DUTTON WAVED BONNIE over to her computer screen.

"What?" Irritated at being interrupted from her work, Bonnie pushed her glasses up on her nose and stared over at her friend.

"You gotta see this," Paige said breathlessly.

Sighing, Bonnie scooted her rolling chair over to Paige's computer screen. She'd been back at work for two days. Once she'd had her revelation in the hypnotist's office, she'd gone straight home.

Since they'd believed Bonnie was on vacation, her family hadn't even missed her. The only problem was, she was no longer satisfied with her dull, drab life, watching movies and digging in her backyard garden. She'd changed.

And even though things hadn't worked out between her and Kurt, she had learned that it *was* possible to find love.

The second time around, however, Bonnie vowed not to lose her identity in the process.

"Pay attention," Paige chided. "This is important."

"What is it? I've got work to do."

"Just look at this."

Bonnie waved a hand.

Paige swiveled her computer screen toward Bonnie. A Facebook ad? "Cinderella, where are you?"

"So what?"

"Hush a minute, will you. Now, where was I? Oh yeah." Paige cleared her throat. "Prince Charming desperately seeking the Elizabeth Destiny look-alike who stole his heart."

"What?" An icy shiver skipped down Bonnie's spine. Was it possible? Kurt wanted her?

Paige nodded. "Yes," she squealed, "can you believe it? There's more."

"Go on." Bonnie leaned forward and squinted at the screen, her heart sprinting at an alarming rate.

"Cinderella, Prince Charming begs your forgiveness. He realizes he's made a very big mistake. If you're interested, please text 550-550-6763." Paige laid the back of her hand across her forehead. "I think I'm going to swoon."

Home. To the ranch. Kurt had taken out a Facebook ad, begging her to forgive him. Impossible.

"Let me see that." Bonnie pushed Paige away from the screen.

Paige clasped a hand over her chest. "Oh, Bonnie, this is so romantic. I bet you never thought getting hit on the head would land you one of the most eligible bachelors in the country."

Shocked, Bonnie read the Facebook ad again. Her hands trembled; her mouth grew dry, and she felt sick to her stomach.

"So when are you leaving?" Paige asked.

"Leaving?"

"You know, to go to Prince Charming."

Bonnie turned back to her own computer. "I'm not."

"What?" Paige's jaw dropped. "How can you turn down something this great?"

"He doesn't love me."

"For crying out loud, the man has asked you to forgive him in a Facebook ad for all the world to see. Do you know how much that must have cost him?"

"I don't care."

"Wait a minute. You've got to give me a better explanation than that. You've been moping around the office ever since you got back. It's obvious you're crazy about the man." Paige grasped Bonnie by the shoulders and stared her in the face.

"Don't you see, he doesn't even know me."

"Oh, please, you lived at his house for ten days!"

"He thought I was Elizabeth Destiny."

"So what? Now he knows you're not."

"He doesn't know the real me. He has no idea who Bonnie Bradford is."

"So teach him."

"I can't, Paige. I'm in over my head."

"What?" Paige smacked her forehead with an open palm. "You're hopeless, Bradford, hopeless."

"Paige, he's expecting someone slick and accomplished like Elizabeth Destiny. Don't you see? I can never compete with a movie star. For heaven's sake, Paige, I'm dull. I'm inexperienced with men, and I watch movies for excitement. How could I possibly hold the interest of a man like Kurt McNally?"

"I don't believe this."

"Please, let's not discuss it anymore."

Paige threw her arms in the air. "Fine. If you want to be the biggest fool on the earth, be my guest."

"Can I get back to work?" Bonnie struggled hard to keep unshed tears from tracking down her cheeks.

Since that moment in the hypnotist's office when her memory had returned, she'd known she wasn't the type of woman who could maintain Kurt's attention. Not for very long. He needed someone worldly, sophisticated, elegant.

Bonnie Bradford was socially inept. She could never move in his circles. She didn't know a salad fork from a soup spoon. Sooner or later, he'd grow bored with an uncultured woman like her. It was much more practical to hide her pain and pretend she'd never seen that ad. Much easier to let go for his sake, even though her heart yearned for him.

"If you let this man get away, you deserve to be an old maid," Paige snapped.

"You don't understand."

"Oh, yes, I do. I understand perfectly. You bury yourself in movies and gardening. You hide from men, from involvement. Face facts, Bonnie Bradford, you're afraid to live."

❧ 18 ❧

Kurt fidgeted. Straightening his tie, he glanced at the clock. Ten thirty. She should be here at any moment. Clearing his throat, he toyed with a pencil on his desk. He'd canceled all his morning appointments for this meeting with the woman he'd come to know as Beth.

The past few days had been a nightmare. He'd gotten over a hundred calls, women all eager to be his Cinderella. Each time the phone had rung, his heart had scaled his throat and his palms had gone sweaty. Each letdown had sent adrenaline bouncing around his system. It had been hell on his nerves.

Then, last night, *she'd* called. He'd recognized her soft voice immediately. His heart had done cartwheels as he invited her to come by his office. He'd ordered ten dozen red roses, one for each day he'd known her. They sat in ten large crystal vases next to a box of chocolates tied in a blue satin ribbon and a bottle of iced champagne.

"Mr. McNally." His secretary buzzed him over the intercom. "Your appointment is here to see you."

"Send her in, Phyllis."

Kurt pushed back his chair and got to his feet. He

planned to sweep her into his arms and kiss her silly. Feeling incredibly excited, he waited.

The door opened, and *she* swept into the room.

"Hello, Kurt," she said.

He took a step forward, his body trembling. "I missed you so much. You don't know how sorry I am for the way I treated you."

"You're forgiven," she purred.

He stepped closer, his heart thumping. An exotic oriental scent teased his nose. Kurt frowned and cocked his head. Something was off.

"Are these all for me?" she cried, pointing at the gifts on his desk.

He nodded, confused by the odd sensation washing through him. Something wasn't right. The long, blond hair was the same, the voice, the blue eyes, but she was different, too, in many subtle ways.

"I'm glad you saw the Facebook ad," he said, studying her closely. "I was so afraid you wouldn't. I targeted it as best I could."

She bent to sniff the roses in one of the ten vases. "These are glorious, Kurt, thank you so much."

"So," Kurt said, leaning against the desk. "Did you get your memory back? Do you know who you really are?"

Her eyes widened guilelessly. "No."

"Where are your glasses?"

"Glasses?" She blinked. "Oh, yes, silly me. I forgot them."

And then he knew with absolute certainty the woman in front of him was the real Elizabeth Destiny.

The cold, calculating woman who'd wounded his pride. But she had never broken his heart because he'd never loved her. Beth had shown him kindness, honesty, and respect, and the contrast was as startling as the difference between sterling silver flatware and disposable plastic utensils.

"Cut the charade, Elizabeth. I know it's you."

"Whatever do you mean?" She splayed one hand across her chest in a dramatic gesture.

Elizabeth and "Beth" might look alike, but that was where all similarity ended. Personality-wise, they were exact opposites. He couldn't believe he had ever mistaken them.

Elizabeth's movements were flamboyant and carefully choreographed to get attention. She swept her arms and tossed her hair and batted her eyelashes. Kurt much preferred Beth's quiet, circumspect countenance. The woman he knew as Beth exuded a calm inner peace whereas Elizabeth Destiny came across as grasping and desperate.

"I know a phony when I see it." Kurt growled.

Her eyes narrowed. "Phony? Me?" She tossed her head. "Darling, I'm the *genuine* Elizabeth Destiny."

"Yeah, I know."

"You've got it bad for me, Kurt. Admit it. Why else would you advertise for my look-alike? It's quite pathetic, really. Thank God, you didn't use your name in that ad. I would have died from embarrassment."

He snorted. "It's unbelievable that I ever mistook *her* for you."

Elizabeth crossed the room, a predatory smile on her face.

Kurt found himself backing up until he bumped into the wall.

She touched him on the arm.

He flinched.

"Why settle for a second-rate imitation when you could have the best?" She walked two fingers up his arm.

His anger flared. Elizabeth had no right to come waltzing in here, trying to claim his affections, calling his mystery girl "second-rate." His "Beth" was the warmest, gentlest, most generous woman he'd ever met, and he would not allow this shallow movie actress to besmirch her.

Roughly, Kurt shoved Elizabeth's hand away. "Get out."

"Is that any way to treat a lady?" She waggled a finger under his nose.

"There's no lady in this room." It took every ounce of control he possessed not to physically toss her out the door.

Elizabeth arched an eyebrow and coolly walked over to the desk. "Roses, chocolates, champagne. Doing it up big, aren't we?"

Furious, he clenched his jaw and glared.

"When you proposed to me, you took me to that tacky little lake."

Kurt winced. He hated to be reminded of his folly. Asking Elizabeth Destiny to marry him had probably been one of the more stupid things he'd done in the course of his thirty-four years. It was time to make amends.

Forcefully, he stalked toward her, grasped her elbow firmly in his hand, and dragged her to the door.

"Get out and don't *ever* come back." He maneuvered her into the hallway.

"Hey! You can't do this to me. I'm Elizabeth Destiny!"

Kurt glanced at his secretary, Phyllis, who was staring at them from her desk in the corner. "Call security."

Elizabeth rolled her eyes. "Fine. If that's the way you want it. No need to get nasty."

"I mean it." He shook an index finger at her. "Don't come back."

Haughtily, she raised her chin. "As if I wanted a peach farmer."

"Then why did you even show up here today?"

She laughed. "I was bored. I thought it might be fun to pretend to be your Cinderella. But you managed to spoil everything."

"Good." Kurt straightened the lapels on his suit, turned his back on the actress, and returned to his office. Closing the door behind him, he dusted his fingers together. "Good riddance to bad rubbish."

Plunking down behind his desk, he stared at the roses, their sweet scent filling his nose, sadness filling his heart.

"Mr. McNally?" Phyllis asked over the intercom.

"Is Elizabeth Destiny still here?" he growled.

"No, sir."

"Oh. What is it, Phyllis?"

"You have a call on line two. A young lady named Paige Dutton. She says she knows who Cinderella is."

"Thank you, Phyllis." Kurt lunged forward, his finger stabbing the blinking light on the telephone. "Hello!"

"Er, is this Prince Charming?" the woman on the other end asked.

"I'm the man who took out the ad, yes."

"My name's Paige Dutton and..."

Kurt could not bear the suspense. "You know Cinderella?"

"Yes."

Joy, overwhelming and complete, expanded Kurt's lungs like helium. "Who is she, where is she? Tell me."

"That's what I'm trying to do." Paige laughed.

"Why didn't she call me herself?"

"Well, that's why I'm calling. See, there's a problem."

"Problem?" Kurt sank back in his chair, his heart skipping frantically.

"It's silly really, and I've tried to convince her otherwise, but you've got to know Bonnie. She's a bit shy."

"Bonnie?"

"My friend, Bonnie Bradford. She's a dead ringer for Elizabeth Destiny."

Bonnie. What a beautiful name! And it fit her perfectly. *Bonnie.* He repeated it to himself. *Bonnie.*

"Tell me about her," he said.

"She got her memory back."

"That's wonderful. Does she still remember me?" Anxiety tightened his gut.

"Yes."

"And...?"

"She doesn't think she's good enough for you."

"What!"

"Silly, I know. I mean if you love someone, it doesn't matter if they're not rich or they are a quiet homebody, does it?"

Love? Bonnie loved him? Hope filled every cell in his body.

"Where is she?" Kurt demanded, fisting one hand.

"At work."

"Where?" He wanted to crawl through the phone and drag the words from Paige's throat. Instead, he picked up a pencil and waited.

Paige gave him the address. Miraculously, it was only three blocks from his office. The whole time Bonnie had been just down the road.

"Thank you, Miss Dutton."

"Hey, I did it for Bonnie. It's about time she had a good man."

Without even taking time to say goodbye, Kurt hung up the phone. He tucked the chocolate box under one arm and grabbed one vase of roses with his other hand.

"I'm going out," he shouted to Phyllis as he zoomed through the lobby and struggled to punch the elevator button.

Bonnie, he thought. Bonnie, Bonnie, Bonnie.

By the time he reached the street, he was running. People stared, but he didn't care. Only one thing dominated his mind —to get to the woman he'd quickly grown to love, beg her forgiveness, and ask her to give him a shot.

Panting, he entered the building at the address Paige had

given him. His palms were so slick with perspiration, he almost dropped the vase of roses.

The elevator slid to the ground floor with a muted *ping*. Kurt got on it, feeling strangely surreal. Blood whooshed in his ears. His knees shook. His stomach twisted.

Bonnie. Exiting the elevator, he marched down the corridor.

A receptionist greeted him. "May I help you, sir?"

"Bonnie Bradford, please."

"I'm sorry, sir, she's in a meeting with Mr. Briggs. Would you like to leave a message?"

Kurt saw Mr. Briggs's name on the door behind them. "Nope," he replied, smiling pleasantly. "I think I'll just pop in and see her right now."

"Sir"—the receptionist got to her feet—"you can't go in there."

"Watch me." He winked. Without missing a beat, he moved past the desk and opened the door marked *Mr. Briggs*.

An older man sat at a desk, talking to Bonnie who was taking notes. He looked up, surprised.

Bonnie was hunched over her notebook computer, her blond hair pulled up in a bun. She didn't see him at first.

Kurt caught his breath.

"May we help you?" Mr. Briggs asked.

"Sir, my name's Kurt McNally, and I'd like a moment alone with your secretary."

"Kurt McNally, the billionaire philanthropist?" Respect and admiration flickered across the lawyer's face.

"Yes, sir."

Kurt noticed Bonnie's hand had frozen in midair, suspended above her notepad. Slowly, she turned her head to look at him, those endearing glasses perched on the end of her nose.

Her eyes met his, and Kurt's heart melted.

"Will this take long?" Mr. Briggs asked, getting to his feet.

"That all depends on Bonnie," Kurt said, his eyes never leaving her sweet, dear face.

Mr. Briggs tapped his watch. "Five minutes, Ms. Bradford."

"Could you make that ten?" Kurt asked.

Mr. Briggs nodded and left the office, the door clicking closed behind him.

"WH...WH...WHAT ARE YOU DOING HERE?" BONNIE stammered. She eyed the roses and the box of chocolates, and her pulse started hammering wildly. Her eyes drank in the sight of him.

"These are for you." He set the gifts down on the desk.

"Thank you," Bonnie said, feeling swept off her feet.

"That's not all."

"No?"

"Bonnie Bradford, I know things happened fast between us, but I want a real shot with you. I want to *be* with you."

"Me?"

"You."

"But you don't even know me."

"I know you better in ten days than I ever knew Elizabeth Destiny in a year of being engaged."

"I'm not her."

"I know. *You're* the one I want."

Stunned, Bonnie simply stared. The whole scene was like something from a romantic movie.

"Bonnie," he said, sinking to his knees in front of her and taking her hand. "I love you."

She tugged her hand from his and dropped her eyes to her lap. She'd waited so long to have a man profess his love for her. But she could not agree to the arrangement. Not until Bonnie was sure she was the woman Kurt truly loved. She could not, would not, live in another woman's shadow.

"I can't," she whispered.

Looking as if she'd slapped him, Kurt rocked back on his heels. "I understand. I came on too strong. I shouldn't have told you I loved you so soon."

"No, oh no! I love you too. With all my heart."

"Then what did I do wrong?" He kneeled in front of her, his eyes searching her face.

"You don't even know *me*."

"Yes, I do. You're the kindest, most honest, most sincere woman I've ever met. Bonnie Bradford, you're the woman I've been searching for my entire life."

"You thought I was Elizabeth Destiny."

"A foolish mistake on my part."

"I fear she's the one you really love."

Kurt threw back his head and laughed.

"Why are you laughing at me?" she asked, wounded.

"Honey." He took her hand in his again, rubbing it tenderly. "Do you know what she did?"

Bonnie shook her head.

"She came to my office pretending to be *you*. She saw my ad on Facebook. I knew very quickly that she wasn't you, and I threw her out of my office."

"You did?"

"Yes. Bonnie, no one smells like you, all strawberries and cream. Your hair feels like spun silk. In my arms, you're soft and real. Bonnie Bradford, you're the woman I love. I can't wait to start discovering every little thing about you."

"I'm not rich," she said, "or glamorous. I'm not cultured or well versed in world affairs."

"Those things aren't important to me."

"Really?"

"I want you to share my home, my heart, my love. I want to build a future with you, Bonnie, and I'll do everything in my power to make you happy." He caressed her palm with his thumb.

What woman could resist?

Bonnie looked into those hazel eyes and knew what she'd known the first time he'd walked into that hospital room. This man was her soul mate. Her better half. The yang to her yin. She had, at last, found her home.

A joy unlike anything she'd ever felt bubbled inside her. The experience was so much richer than any romantic movie scene she'd ever watched.

"Yes," she said and wrapped her arms around him. The man she'd thought lost to her forever.

"Bonnie, my love, I'll make you the happiest woman on earth." He pulled her out of the chair and into his arms.

They sat on the floor, entwined in each other's arms. Kurt rained kisses like snowflakes on her nose, her cheek, her chin, her eyelashes.

Bonnie inhaled his scent, burrowed into his arms, and sighed her contentment. Then his mouth caught hers, and he took her straight to paradise.

"Well, Cinderella," he said, several minutes later. "It seems the shoe fits."

"A very comfortable fit," she agreed.

"How's your head?" Kurt lightly fingered the area on her temple where she'd been struck by the board.

"Fine."

"From now on, you're going to have to avoid getting hit on the head."

"Oh." Bonnie stared, mesmerized by this man. "And why is that?"

"I don't want you to ever forget who I am."

"No?" she teased. "Wait a minute, my memory is getting fuzzy. What did you say your name was?"

"Prince Charming," he drawled, his mouth lowering to hers again. "And don't you ever forget it."

DEAR READER, I HOPE YOU HAVE ENJOYED, *KURT*.

If you have the time, I would so appreciate a review. Just a couple of words will do. Thank you so much for leaving a review. You are appreciated!

If you would like to read more Texas Rascals, the latest book in the series is *Tucker*.

For an excerpt please turn the page.

Much love, Lori Wilde

Visit Lori on the Web @ Lori Wilde. Sign up for news of Lori's releases @ Lori's newsletter

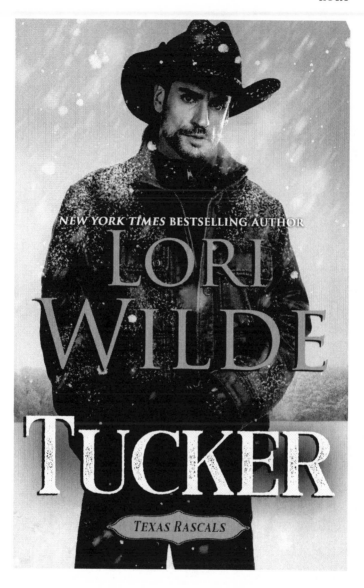

NEW YORK TIMES BESTSELLING AUTHOR

LORI WILDE

TUCKER

TEXAS RASCALS

CHAPTER—TUCKER EXCERPT

There he was again.

July Johnson peered out her second-story kitchen window at the scruffy fellow in a worn leather jacket lounged against her brick apartment building.

Underneath his black cowboy hat, shaggy dark hair, three months past the point of needing a trim, curled down his collar. His faded jeans were threadbare, and several days' beard growth ringed his jaw. His shabby cowboy boots were dirty.

He'd been lurking around her small apartment complex in Rascal, Texas for several days. She spotted him each morning when she woke up, then again before she went to bed. She decided that he was either he was a thief casing a place to rob or a homeless man seeking shelter.

July frowned. Perhaps she should call someone's attention to the situation. Unfortunately, the apartment manager didn't reside on-site.

There was sweet Mrs. O'Brien who lived below her, but July didn't want to alarm the elderly lady unnecessarily. The Kirkwoods, a young married couple, occupied the apartment next to hers but they both worked an early-morning shift at the hospital.

Running a hand through her short curls, July considered going across the courtyard and knocking on the new tenants' door, but something about those two men bothered her.

The Stravanos brothers weren't very approachable. They never returned her greetings and rarely smiled. Frequently she'd witnessed them arguing. They kept odd hours and often entertained a parade of unsavory characters.

Come to think of it, maybe the guy in the alley was a friend of theirs. He seemed their type.

July stood on her tiptoes, planted both palms on the counter and leaned forward for a closer look, her nose pressing flat against the windowpane.

Despite his "down-on-your-luck" appearance, the man was undeniably gorgeous. The way he carried himself intrigued her. He moved with the controlled grace of an athlete—fluid, confident, imperturbable. Heck, he even slouched sexily.

The November wind gusted, swirling debris into the air. The man turned up his collar. Something about him put July in mind of country singer Brad Paisley.

Her heart beat a little faster. Oh, come on, she couldn't be attracted to him, for heaven's sake. He was indigent, or worse.

Immediately contrite for her unkind thoughts, she chided herself. Now, July Desiree, you of all people should know you can't make snap judgments. Everyone deserves the benefit of a doubt.

Dormant memories of her troubled childhood flitted through July's mind. She shook her head. Personal experience taught her that anyone could be redeemed. Even the most desperate cases. All it took was for one person to care. Just one loving individual who would offer calm patience and unconditional acceptance.

The man ambled over to the Dumpster wedged beside a chain-link fence and disappeared from her view.

Hmm, where had he gone?

Placing one knee on the counter, she had to crane her neck at an odd angle to see him.

He cast a furtive glance right, then left. Satisfied no one was observing him, he bent over and rummaged inside the garbage bin, favoring July with a glimpse of his backside.

Goodness. July gulped and laid a palm across her chest. What a glorious tush.

He searched for several minutes. Finally, shaking his head, the man straightened and dusted his hands against the seat of his jeans.

What was he looking for? Was the poor cowboy so hungry, he'd been reduced to pillaging the Dumpster for food? Her heart wrenched and her natural crusading instincts kicked into overdrive. Nothing captured July's interest quicker than a worthy cause.

And this guy had "cause" written all over him in neon letters.

He was a proverbial diamond in the rough. Despite his rocky demeanor, July saw something special shining through. Shave him, shower him, dress him in new clothing, and July would bet her last nickel he'd be a regular male version of Eliza Doolittle.

He squinted up at her window.

Their eyes met.

Startled, July jumped, lost her balance and tumbled forward into the sink. Her elbow contacted with a plastic, liquid soap dispenser and knocked it to the floor.

One leg flailed wildly in the air. Her breast brushed against the water faucet, accidentally turning the handle.

"Oh, oh," she gasped as cold water soaked her sweater.

Teeth chattering, she wrenched off the faucet and extricated herself from the stainless-steel sink. Muttering under her breath, she took the time to sop up spilled soap before stripping off her sweater and dropping it into the laundry basket situated outside the kitchen door.

Earlier, before she'd spotted the stranger, she'd planned to head down to the laundry room and wash a load of clothes. Padding into the bedroom for a fresh sweater, July kept thinking about the man.

He had indeed taken her by surprise, catching her eye like that. For one brief second, they had forged an instant connection.

A connection so unexpected, it sent her head reeling. Even now, remembering his intense eyes, she felt slightly breathless.

"It's the cold water, you ninny," she said out loud. "That's all."

So why did she hurry back to the kitchen and sidle over to the window again? Curiosity, July assured herself. Nothing more. She wanted to know who this man was and why he lurked in her alley.

Curiosity killed the cat, July Johnson.

If she had a dime for every time her family or friends had teased her with that phrase, she would be a wealthy woman.

"Satisfaction brought him back," she said out loud, inching aside the yellow lace curtains.

She peeked out.

The alley yawned empty.

The man had vanished.

"Damn," Tucker Haynes swore. "Damn, damn, damn."

He jammed his hands into his jacket. Hunching his shoulders against the wind, he stalked down the alley. Tucker was disgruntled. The package of stolen credit cards hadn't been in the Dumpster as his informant, Duke Petruski, had promised him they would be.

Tucker smelled of garbage, and to top things off, some nosy Rosy in that upstairs apartment had been spying on him.

He'd seen her for just the briefest of moments, but it had been long enough for Tucker to realize he'd been spotted. His impression was one of a wide-eyed young female with a short cap of sandy brown curls.

A very cute female.

Their gazes had held for a second, then she'd disappeared from the window. Had he blown his cover already?

Maybe, Tucker hoped, she'd believe what he wanted her to believe—that he was a homeless transient digging for discarded treasures in the Dumpster—and go about her business. In the meantime, common sense urged him out of the alley. He'd get to a phone, see if he could rouse Petruski and find out what had gone wrong.

Tucker rounded the building, but he heard an apartment door slam and stopped cold. Pressing his back against the brick wall, he inched forward, his ears intently attuned, his muscles tensed.

Angry male voices buzzed in a low hum. Tucker clenched his jaw and moved closer, straining to hear the conversation.

"That's no excuse," said one angry man.

"What do you want me to do about it?" The second speaker had a deeper voice. More gravel and gall.

"Find out what happened to those credit cards. They didn't just disappear into thin air. Somebody took them."

"It isn't that simple."

Tucker reached the edge of the building. Steeling himself for flight if he was discovered, he quickly poked his head around the corner.

Two men stood arguing in the courtyard thirty feet from where Tucker lurked.

Big, beefy, ugly.

The two claimed ruddy complexions, massive hands, and wide feet. They were his quarry all right, the much sought-after Stravanos brothers, known to the El Paso Police Department as the resident kings of credit card fraud.

Tucker had been tracking them for over a month before he'd finally located them three days ago in this tiny apartment complex In Rascal, Texas. This time they would not elude capture as they had on numerous past occasions. This time, Tucker Haynes would be the one to nail their hides to the wall.

The older Stravanos, Leo, waved a burly fist underneath his brother's bulbous nose.

"Don't threaten me," Mikos Stravanos growled.

"It is not a threat, little brother, it is a promise. Get me answers, or it's your skin."

Tucker smiled. Looks like Duke Petruski had stirred up a hornet's nest. Good. He wanted the brothers at each other's throats.

"Excuse me?"

At the gentle touch of a hand on his shoulder, Tucker leaped a foot and plastered himself flat against the wall, palms splayed across the cold bricks, his heart galloping.

Tucker stared at the petite brunette standing beside him.

Good gosh almighty, the woman had snuck up on him! What kind of police detective was he, letting his concentration slip?

"What do you want, lady?" he growled, trying hard to recoup his composure.

Her wide green eyes grew even rounder. "Why, to help you, of course."

Help him? Did she know something about the Stravanos brothers? Startled, Tucker just kept staring.

"I saw you digging in the Dumpster," she explained, sympathy written on her heart-shaped face. "And I wanted you to know that I understand your situation."

Ah, the nosy Rosy.

"I appreciate your concern." He forced a smile. "But it's completely unnecessary."

He had to get rid of her fast and find out what was going on between the Stravanos brothers. Cocking his head, he listened. They were still arguing.

"There's nothing to be ashamed of," the girl continued, her voice soft and gentle.

"You think I'm ashamed?" Tucker shifted his attention back to her.

"Falling on hard times can be a blow to the ego, but don't let it make you bitter. Anyone can overcome a bad experience. All it takes is one step in the right direction."

"Me? Bitter?" He raised an eyebrow and smirked.

Who was this inquisitive little sprite? A blast of air whipped her hair into a mad tousle, giving her a sexy windblown appearance.

The twin hard bumps rising beneath her sweater signaled that she was cold. Tucker had a sudden urge to wrap his arms around those slender shoulders and warm her.

"Everyone needs a helping hand now and then," she said, continuing her soothing pep talk.

"Excuse me, lady, but what do you want?" he asked, trying his best not to stare point-blank at her chest.

"I thought you might like to have breakfast with me," she invited, her grin engulfing her whole face.

"Huh?"

"In my apartment. I was about to make oatmeal and scrambled eggs. You look hungry."

"Lady, I'm a stranger to you."

Her gaze swept his ragged clothes. She pursed her lips. Very lovely lips at that, Tucker noted.

"We're all brothers in God's eyes," she said quietly.

Whew boy, he'd drawn himself a real goody-two-shoes. Tucker was just about to tell her to get lost when he heard the Stravanos brothers walking from the courtyard toward the parking lot where he and the girl stood. He could not afford to be spotted. Suddenly her invitation seemed like a godsend.

Quickly he took her arm. "Breakfast? Sounds great. Which one is your apartment?"

He cast a worried glance over his shoulder, then searched the row of windows above them as he guided her toward the alley.

"We could go through the courtyard," she offered, gesturing in that direction.

"I'd rather go in the way you came out." He tugged her into the alley and breathed a sigh of relief.

"Follow me," she said, leading him through the rear entrance.

Feeling edgy, Tucker ran a hand along the back of his neck. He trailed behind her as she ascended the stairs. Her hips swayed enticingly, and he couldn't help noticing how her blue jeans molded to her well-portioned fanny. Unbidden, the image of that derriere completely unclothed rose in his mind.

Knock it off, Haynes. This certainly isn't the time or place for lascivious thoughts. But something about her defied his best intentions. It ought to be against the law for the woman to wear tight jeans.

"By the way," she chattered, stopping on the landing and pulling keys from her pocket. "My name's July Johnson, what's yours?"

"Tucker Haynes," he replied before realizing he probably shouldn't have revealed his real name.

"Well, Tucker, it's a real pleasure to meet you." She smiled so widely, he wondered if the action hurt her mouth. Looping the key ring around the index finger of her left hand, she extended her right in a confident gesture of camaraderie.

Caught off guard by her relentless friendliness, he shook her hand.

Her palm was warm and soft, and he registered that she did not wear a wedding band. His heart lightened while his gut tightened. He wanted, suddenly, to take care of her.

How did she do it, he wondered. Offer a strange homeless man unconditional acceptance? Not smart. But he couldn't be charmed by her guilelessness.

Disguised like a transient cowboy as he was, Tucker had been on the receiving end of some harsh responses. Most people turned up their noses, refusing him service in restaurants, called him derogatory names or worse. He didn't expect anything else.

The treatment wasn't much different from what he'd grown accustomed to as a kid. Tucker Haynes, just another punk from the wrong side of the tracks. As a result of the slings and arrows, he'd suffered in his childhood Tucker had never been able to take anyone at face value.

He hadlearned the hard way that people could not be trusted. Apparently, July Johnson was one of the lucky few. She had not yet rubbed up against that ugly life lesson.

She was too trusting. No attractive young woman should invite a strange man into her home. Ever. Under any circumstances.

And he would never have come up to her apartment if he hadn't been avoiding the Stravanos brothers.

"Here we go," she chirped, opening the door to her apartment and standing aside for him to enter.

Feeling as nervous as rookie cop policing his first political protest, Tucker walked a few steps into the apartment. His gaze swept the living room, sizing up its occupant in a quick once-over.

The sofa was upholstered in a rose tapestry material and adorned with a handmade afghan. Pink, heart-shaped throw pillows decorated the rocking chair. Lush mauve carpeting covered the floor. Figurines lined a glassed-in hutch—kittens, puppies, pigs, elephants, giraffes, lions—a real glass menagerie.

Opposite the window stood a brick fireplace. Thanksgiving decorations adorned the mantel in jubilant fall colors—orange, brown, yellow, red and plastic fruit spilling from a horn of plenty. Straw pilgrim dolls sat beside paper turkeys.

Tucker shifted his gaze, disturbed by the festive atmosphere. He'd never been one for holiday celebrations. To him, the holidays meant only one thing—drunken family brawls that often led to violence, mayhem, and bloodshed.

He batted the thought away and continued his catalog of July's apartment. A large bookcase housed hundreds of romance novels, and a lot of self-help books. An ornate Victorian-style lamp sat on a solid oak coffee table, cream-colored tassels dangling from the shade. Different varieties of dried flowers protruded from various vases placed strategically around the room, and dozens of framed snapshots hung on the walls.

She must have a lot of friends, he thought, noticing how many different people were featured in the photographs. He thought of his own apartment, utterly bare of pictures, and blinked against the sadness moving through him.

July's place was cozy, romantic, friendly. The sort of home that made him uncomfortable.

"Come on in," she invited, moving past him into the kitchen. "I'll get breakfast started."

Tucker cleared his throat. An incredible awkwardness stole over him. Edging to the window, he parted the rose-colored draperies and peered down at the courtyard below.

Damn. The obstinate Stravanos brothers were still standing by the gate arguing. Tucker wondered how they ever managed to pull off the complex crimes they'd committed.

They didn't seem to be all that bright and fought constantly.

He wished the brothers would move on. Now. So he could escape this place.

Running a hand through his hair, Tucker sighed. He had to get the heck out of here before he overdosed on cheerfulness.

ABOUT THE AUTHOR

Lori Wilde is the New York Times, USA Today and Publishers' Weekly bestselling author of 87 works of romantic fiction. She's a three time Romance Writers' of America RITA finalist and has four times been nominated for Romantic Times Readers' Choice Award. She has won numerous other awards as well.

Her books have been translated into 26 languages, with more than four million copies of her books sold worldwide.

Her breakout novel, The First Love Cookie Club, has been optioned for a TV movie.

Lori is a registered nurse with a BSN from Texas Christian University. She holds a certificate in forensics, and is also a certified yoga instructor.

A fifth generation Texan, Lori lives with her husband, Bill, in the Cutting Horse Capital of the World; where they run Epiphany Orchards, a writing/creativity retreat for the care and enrichment of the artistic soul.